PLAYA VISTA SOCIAL CLUB

ZINA PATEL

To my wonderful husband Mel, my lobster and soulmate.

... and to our dear friends and Playa Vista neighbors, who obviously are nothing like these shady characters ... So many good times!

This book is meant to be paired with a chilled glass of chardonnay while sitting in a poolside cabana... please enjoy!

MIA

3 Days Missing

The sun was starting to set over the Los Angeles skyline. My stomach turned at the thought of another day without my best friend. I pulled my cell phone out of my pocket, and was scrolling through hoping that there'd be an update when I got the text. *The police are here.* I didn't think twice before rushing out the door of my apartment so fast I didn't even tell Aaron where I was going. I heard him barreling down the hall after me but I was already in the elevator heading down to the lobby.

The sound of the polished elevator doors sent a chill down the back of my spine as they opened to reveal a lobby full of familiar faces all gawking at me, huddled, and whispering. I felt uneasy, but I knew there had to be someone here that knew something. I rushed over to the police officer who'd been chatting with a few of the other tenants and from the moment they saw me, they backed away. I couldn't understand why, and I glanced around to see that everyone had been talking about me. *They can't possibly think I had something to do with this, can they? Jade is my best friend.*

"Excuse me, officer. Have there been any updates on Jade's whereabouts?"

"Who are you?" he asked, snappily.

"I'm Mia. I'm the one that filed the missing person's report. I spoke to a few of the other officers about this, but I haven't heard anything since. You're here now. Do you know what happened?"

"Are you family?"

"No. She's my best friend and I would like to know what happened to her," I said, unable to hide my frustration.

"I'm not at liberty to discuss what we currently know about this case. Is there anything you can tell me about where she could've gone?"

"I told the police everything I knew about the situation. I was told I'd have an answer by now whether you guys were moving forward with the investigation or not. Look, all I want is for you to bring my best friend home. Is that too much to ask?"

I felt two hands pressing against my shoulders comfortingly and I looked back to see Aaron standing there, trying to get me to back down.

"Ma'am, I'm just trying to put the pieces together here. If anything comes up, the family will be notified."

"But - "

"Let it go, Mia. You aren't going to get any more answers out of him," said Aaron.

I took a deep breath, watching the officer make his way over to David. I squinted at him angrily, wishing I could walk right up to him and demand he tell me where Jade was. *I told the police all about what you've been doing to Jade. I know you're somehow involved in this, David. If the cops aren't going to help me figure this out, I'll just have to do it myself.*

Aaron took me back up to our apartment, helping me settle on the couch before wrapping me up in a blanket. I felt sick to my stomach thinking about where Jade could be right now and what she could be going through. I felt so helpless, and it seemed like the cops weren't interested in listening to what I had to say. *Why aren't they taking this seriously? This is so unlike Jade. She wouldn't just up and leave without telling me. I know she wouldn't.*

"Mia, you need to eat something. You haven't eaten much at all these past few days. I know this is tough, but you can't continue living like this," said Aaron.

"How am I supposed to go on living like everything is just fine, when Jade could be out there suffering through so much and we don't even know it?"

"Look, Mia. I know you're trying to do everything you can here, but you have to remember that Jade has a life behind closed doors. You can't possibly know everything that she was dealing with. You may think she'd never just up and leave, but maybe that's exactly what she did."

"How could you say that, Aaron? You know Jade was building a life here. Playa Vista Towers is her home. The person responsible for this is currently being consoled by the police instead of interrogated," I snapped.

"All I'm saying is that it's too early to tell what exactly happened. Give the cops some time to do their job, okay?"

I sighed, trying to calm myself down, but there were still so many unanswered questions that were taking up space inside my mind. I replayed the last few days before Jade went missing over again in my head trying to figure out what went wrong. *You really made me feel like you had everything under control, Jade. Maybe the situation with David was worse than you made it out to be. If he did hurt you, I hope the police nail him to a wall because if they don't, I'll just have to do it on my own.*

From the moment I gave my statement to the police, I felt like they dismissed it as another problematic marriage debacle. They barely listened when I told them that David was dangerous, that he could've hurt Jade and done so much more, and that made my blood boil. *As if we didn't have enough to deal with being on lockdown in this place. Someone has to know something. If I don't have the answers soon, I really feel like I'm going to lose my mind.*

I didn't quite mind staying at home in the early months of the pandemic. I had time to focus on my writing, get closer to Aaron, and life in Playa Vista Towers felt like its own little world. There was enough to do to keep me from feeling trapped or confined in one space for too long, but now that Jade is missing, that all changed.

I couldn't peel myself away from my laptop, as I remained curled up on the couch for the better part of the day. I looked up to see that the sun was already starting to set and the Los Angeles skyline looked like it was lit up with stars. I remembered how good it felt to be out there having dinner in the open air, chatting with Jade about all that we had going on in our lives. Despite how much Jade had been through, she always managed to keep it together, and that was more than I could've said for myself. *You told me to go after my dreams, but here I am watching each day pass me by hoping you'll somehow come home.*

"Mia, have you been sitting there all day?" asked Aaron. He walked in through the front door of our apartment, placing his keys on the entryway table, giving me that look of pure concern.

"I haven't moved. I don't know how to do anything anymore, Aaron. You saw the way the police are handling this. They really believe that Jade would just leave, without so much as saying goodbye. I feel stuck, like if I stay here long enough, I'll get the call that she's okay," I confessed, feeling a single tear trickle down my face.

"Hey, hey."

Aaron rushed over to my side and I laid my head on his chest, feeling the warmth emanate from him as the scent of his expensive cologne lulled me. He held me tight and I cried for the first time in three days, wishing I knew how to help find my best friend. From the moment I first talked to the police, I had a terrible feeling in the pit of my stomach like they weren't going to honor their word and do whatever it took to bring Jade home. I knew that if I sat around hoping the answers would show up at my door, I'd be waiting a long time.

"Jade would kill you if she saw you like this. She'd want you to go on living your life, Mia. I know you don't trust the cops on this, but what else can you do? It's not like you can find her on your own."

"Maybe I can," I said, feeling a wave of confidence wash over me.

"Mia…"

"Look, Aaron. I don't expect you to understand any of this, but if it were someone you cared deeply about, you'd want to do whatever it took to help them, right?"

He nodded at me, gulping. I could tell that he didn't want me getting involved in this because we still had no idea what we were dealing with. For all we knew, Jade could be in serious danger, but I had a gut feeling that there was a Playa Vista Towers resident that knew what happened to her. *She couldn't have just vanished into thin air. If someone knows where she was the night she disappeared, then I have to find out.*

"I'm worried about you, Mia."

"Don't be. I promise I'll be fine, but you're right. I'm not going to get anywhere by holing up in here."

"That we can both agree on. I want you to know that I'm here for you. I know this is a really tough time, but you have my support. I love you," said Aaron.

I smiled wide, feeling the softness of his lips as I kissed him. "I love you, too."

"How about we head down to *The Vine* for dinner. I can't remember the last time we ordered groceries, and you need to eat something. It's been a while since we had some alone time," he offered.

"I think that sounds wonderful. Let me get changed."

He kissed me softly before I ventured off into the bathroom

to freshen up. I felt so much better knowing that I had Aaron, that we had a strong foundation, and that despite this crazy endeavor I was about to embark on, he was there for me regardless. *After all we've been through, you're the only thing getting me through the day now. I wish I could be doing more for you, for us, and for this family.*

I painted a light wash of pink on my full lips thinking about all of the times Aaron and I'd tried to have a baby. Finding out that I may never be able to give him one shattered me, made me feel like he would eventually fall out of love with me, but he stuck by me through that. *Now, he's sticking by me through this. I really can't ask for anything more.*

~

Aaron and I made our way down to *The Vine*, nestled in the heart of the Playa Vista Towers complex, right across from the courtyard. I could smell the scent of incredible food wafting through the air as the residents clutched their Chanel purses, enjoying their wine, trying to return to a sense of normalcy. It wasn't like many of them seemed to mind the lockdown since they all lived in their own little bubble, enjoying the small boutiques, gym, and restaurants Playa Vista Towers had to offer. It was our own little world that sometimes seemed so big you could get lost in it. Aaron pulled out my chair for me and I hung my purse on the side of it, getting comfortable, trying to enjoy the warm air and candlelight. We placed our order and he stretched his hand across the table, brushing his fingertips along my skin, smiling.

"I know this may not be much to help you through this, but I'm glad we came out tonight," he said.

"It's perfect, Aaron. I didn't realize how badly I needed to get out of the apartment for a little while."

The waiter came around with Aaron's steak and my salmon, topping off our wine before he left. I caught sight of

Laura and Emmanuel enjoying their dinner at a table near us. Laura turned to me smiling, and I waved at her. I could see the worry in her eyes and it dawned on me that she, much like many others dining tonight, were all probably trying to take their mind off of Jade's disappearance. It disrupted the peaceful elegance everyone at Playa Vista Towers seemed to love so much. I knew there were those that absolutely hated that, and then there were those like Laura who simply wished things would go on as they had before. *I feel it too, Laura. Something isn't right here.*

We passed by their table on the way back up to our apartment and as I drew closer, I saw just how distraught the two of them really were. I didn't want to ask any questions, not yet at least, but it was nice to know that I wasn't alone in the way I felt. My stomach turned as I got into bed that night, and it was at that moment I realized that no one was going to fight for Jade the way she deserved. I was the only person she was ever close to, and that meant it was up to me to put the pieces together, otherwise this would just get swept under the rug. *I won't let that happen to you, Jade. We will bring you home. I just need to start asking all the right questions, and hopefully I'll find out the truth soon enough.*

∼

I sat with my coffee at the dining table, scrolling through my emails as Aaron came rushing over for a kiss before he left. He looked as handsome as ever with his light brown hair slicked back and his freshly-pressed suit jacket perfectly tailored to fit.

"I'll see you tonight, Mia. I love you."

"I love you too, Aaron. Have a great day," I told him. He smiled, kissing my forehead before he left. I hated being in the apartment alone because I had far too much time on my hands to think. I sipped on my coffee, going over the new work applications I was getting ready to send out for a remote writing position. Aaron told me time and time again that I didn't have to, that he had plenty of money to take care of us both, but I wanted this more than anything. I wanted to share my stories with the world and relished in the fulfillment of doing something I loved every single day.

Jade and I would always talk about how she couldn't wait to see a book of mine on the shelf of her favorite bookstore and cafe which was hidden on a street corner in downtown LA. We'd promised each other that we'd go back there eventually once the lockdown was lifted and life felt normal again, but now I worried that she may never get that chance. I took a deep breath, trying to relax as another email notification came in, telling me there was a package waiting in the lobby that needed a signature. I ran my fingers through my mess of black hair, tucking it behind my ears before grabbing my keys and heading straight for the elevator.

"Mia, it's nice to see you again. Can you sign here, please?"

"Of course, Victor," I said, taking the pen from him.

I signed on the line, watching as he scrambled behind the desk for my package. He handed it to me, and I smiled, shaking it slightly before I read the label to see where it was from.

"I haven't seen you here in a while. I guess you aren't spending every moment of lockdown scouring the internet for more things to buy, huh?"

"Some of us like shopping a little more than others, I suppose. I'm sure you're probably getting a crazy amount of packages every single day," I said, chuckling.

"Oh, you bet. I nearly threw my back out yesterday carrying them all in."

I was getting ready to head back upstairs when I heard a familiar voice coming from the elevators on the other side of the lobby. There he was, standing in front of me with that fake warmth in his smile, like I wasn't going to tell him exactly how I felt. I rushed over, feeling my cheeks get hot with anger, wishing I could throw my new blender directly at his head. *I know you have something to do with this, David. This is all your fault. It has to be.*

"Mia. I haven't seen you around much," said David.

"You can't be serious. David, your wife is missing. The cops are doing a terrible job conducting this investigation and something tells me you have a hand in that. Don't think I don't know what you've been putting her through. What the hell did you do with my best friend? Huh?"

I was fighting the urge to cry, and he just stared at me blankly, sighing deeply like he didn't expect me to blow up on him like this.

"Mia, I know you're upset, but I would never hurt Jade. I love her."

"You loved her so much you cheated on her? She's had her suspicions for some time, David. You come home drunk every night. You can't possibly expect me to sit back and just believe that this has absolutely nothing to do with you. You better tell the cops where you took her or what you did with her because if she doesn't come home, I will kill you," I threatened, through my teeth.

"I didn't hurt Jade. I know I'm not perfect, Mia. We can't all be like Aaron, okay? Some of us have some deep shit we have to deal with, but I did not hurt her. All I want is to bring her home, too. I'm sorry you can't see that."

He walked right past me, heading straight out the automatic doors to the courtyard for some fresh air. I watched him slip his AirPods in so he wouldn't have to listen to anyone around him, and my stomach started to turn again. For a moment, I wondered if he'd been telling the truth. I saw that look in his eyes, the defeat in his expression, and it only left me feeling more confused. *I will find out what happened, Jade. I will find the person that's responsible for this, and I will bring you home. Is it possible David really wasn't involved? If not him, then who?*

2

DAVID

5 Days Missing

I poured myself another glass of whiskey, hoping it would numb how shitty I felt, but I was still a nervous wreck. It was like I was waiting every second of every day for the cops to pull up and put me in handcuffs, read me my rights, tell me they found some shit that was enough to arrest me for Jade's disappearance. *Jade, where the fuck did you go? Huh? This whole damn complex thinks I'm responsible for this. Your best friend thinks I'm the reason you disappeared, but I'm not. If you left my ass because you were tired of me, you should've said something.*

I could barely get any damn sleep, tossing and turning, waiting for the next call that would give me an update on where the hell she was. I always kept tabs on her, made sure she wasn't doing anything stupid to make me look bad. This shit was the worst possible thing she could've done. Part of me wondered if something bad had happened to her, but I settled on the fact she probably just up and left because she couldn't take my shit anymore. *That ain't like you to leave without at least telling Mia. You're still in town because the airports are closed, Jade.*

The cops are going to find you somewhere, and they better. I'm tired of dealing with this shit.

I knocked out for a while right there on the living room couch. When I woke up, I was drenched in sweat again. I was having dreams of being thrown in jail for this, and I knew that could become a damn reality any day now with the cops building a case against me. As much as I wanted to forget this even happened, I couldn't. I needed to figure out where the fuck Jade went before the cops did because there was no way in hell I was letting them pin this shit on me.

I got up and made my way to the fridge to grab a cold beer and a slice of pizza from five days ago. It was the last thing Jade ordered before she went missing, and I hated to admit it, but it was a pain to eat knowing that. I washed it down with the beer, trying to pull myself together long enough to figure out how I was going to work tomorrow morning. I needed a distraction, something to keep me preoccupied so I wouldn't be worrying nonstop. My phone screen lit up in the darkness.

I grabbed it to see a text come in from Irina, the self-proclaimed leader of our little clique, the Playa Vista Social Club. *We're having dinner tomorrow night. It was Serge's idea. A bunch of the others are coming. I hope to see you there.* The last thing I wanted was to be around the rest of them, but I knew the whispers and the rumors would get worse if I decided not to show my face.

I texted her back before I turned in for the night, getting an hour of sleep before the sun came up. I could already hear my phone blowing up with email notifications. I sighed, dragging myself into the shower, letting the hot water wash away some of the frustration I felt before getting ready to spend the entire day sitting at my desk, working my ass off. I made myself a cup of coffee, hopping on a work call, and before I knew it the day was slowly passing me by. Every time I had a minute to myself I was constantly checking my phone to see if I had any missed calls from the cops, but there was nothing. I breathed a sigh of relief each time.

Getting through the rest of my workday, I looked forward to having some of that expensive liquor Serge's got locked away in his cabinet. *That isn't the only thing of his I've taken,* I thought, pulling out my best dress shirt and cologne for this thing so the rest of the crew wouldn't think I was losing my shit. I knew I was probably going to be answering a lot of questions tonight, dealing with the whispers, and the inevitable side-eyeing, but I didn't care. There was no way I'd be able to convince a bunch of rich assholes that I wasn't involved in my wife's disappearance, at least not yet.

I took one last look at myself in the mirror near the front door before I left, locking the door behind me. It felt strange not to have Jade on my arm for this, because I swore it was the times we were around everyone else that we seemed to get along the best. *We could've fixed this shit, Jade. All you had to do was talk to me.* I couldn't remember the last time we had a real conversation. It was like we didn't know each other anymore, like we became two damn strangers, and that made our marriage an absolute nightmare. There was a time we were happy, *really* happy, but that boat sailed a long time ago.

Now, I just wanted her back so everyone would shut up about this. On my way to Irina's front door, I was retracing my steps of the night Jade supposedly went missing, but I still couldn't figure out what the hell happened. *I better figure this shit out soon before it comes to bite me in the ass.*

"Well, look who it is. Come on in, David," said Irina.

She looked absolutely stunning with her platinum blonde hair pulled back into a low bun and her lips a perfect shade of red. I could practically feel how soft they were, wishing I could whisk her off to her bedroom like I'd done so many times before. *Not when the husband's home, or at least that's what she likes to say.*

"Thank you for having me."

She opened the door wide and I caught a glimpse of Serge looking at me like he wanted to pummel me in the doorway. I smiled, catching everyone's heads turned to look at me, staring like they were watching a trainwreck waiting to happen.

"It's nice to see you, David. I'm glad you could come out tonight," said Karen.

She twirled a strand of her hair with a glass of wine in hand, leading me over to the bar so I could get a drink of my own. She talked my ear off about all of the shit she was dealing with and how she couldn't wait to stick it to Tony the moment she had the chance. I pretended to hang onto every word because if I didn't, she'd be the first to be talking to everyone about how I seemed strange or distant even though my wife vanished into thin air. I sighed, taking the moment she went to get us another set of drinks to talk to someone else before we all sat down for dinner.

"Hey, man. I just wanted to say I'm sorry for what you're going through. I also should apologize for how Mia acted. She should've never come at you like that," said Aaron, patting me on the back.

"Hey, don't worry about it. Mia's dealing with a lot, too. I can understand her wanting to blame me, because that's what everyone seems to do in these situations," I murmured.

"Not everyone thinks you're guilty, David. Trust me. There are some of us that are just hoping Jade returns home safely."

"Thank you, Aaron. Hey, where is Mia tonight?"

"She thought it best to sit this one out. She's trying her best to return to life as normal, but I mean normal really isn't possible anymore, is it? She's still in shock, but she'll come around. She won't be jumping down your throat about this again."

"It's alright if she does. I'm a big boy. I can take it," I responded, with a chuckle.

It wasn't long before Irina was calling us all into her grand dining room that she'd just had redecorated for the third time because there simply wasn't anything else for her to do. Sasha was at her mother's for the night, and I could already tell she was glad for the break. Irina wasn't the kind of woman that naturally had a motherly instinct, but she tried her best. She did what she could to keep her interesting family dynamic intact, even though she and Serge were often at each other's throats. *That never stopped me from sleeping with her. Maybe I started sleeping with her because of it. She's always been a good time.*

I pulled out my chair, taking a seat just as the catering staff brought out the first course. I tried to focus on the food, but I could barely get through it with everyone glancing over at me when they thought I wasn't looking, probably gathering enough to fuel tomorrow's elevator gossip. Once we made it to the third course I was sure I was in the clear of any comments, but that's when Serge decided to step in. He tapped his spoon on his glass to get everyone's attention, and we all turned to look at him sitting proudly at the head of the table.

"I wanted to thank you all for joining us this evening. I know it's been a crazy year for us all, and it seems to be getting crazier by the minute, but I'm just glad we all have each other. When this lockdown is over and we're all back to our normal lives, we have to remember this time. We may never be this close again."

"Here's to that," Aaron chimed in.

We all raised our glasses, but that's when I caught Serge looking directly at me, and I knew his speech wasn't over yet.

"I also wanted to say that I hope you're doing alright, David. We all know how difficult this must be for you, and we hope that Jade finds her way home safely. If there's anything you need, we need you to know that we're all here for you," he said.

It was a nice sentiment, but I knew it was far from the truth where he was concerned. That man hated my guts from the first time I met him and his wife when they moved into Playa Vista Towers. They were so full of life, wrapped up in each other like they really did love each other at some point, but that quickly changed once their differences started to show.

Irina was a narcissistic brat parading around like she owned the place and Serge tried to assert his dominance every chance he got. It was one hell of a sight to see when I was standing on the sidelines, but now that I was in bed with Irina, it was like Serge was waiting for the right time to nail my ass to the wall.

"Thank you, Serge. Thank you all," I said, raising my glass again as everyone joined in.

I downed my drink fast, right as one of the staff came around to top it off, but Serge stopped her.

"He's had enough. You can bring him some water," he said, slyly.

Cutting me off this early, are you? Why am I not surprised? It was from that moment on I couldn't wait to get out of there because getting through the night without a good drink in my hand felt impossible. Once it was time to leave, Irina came over, brushing my shoulder with her fingertips, pulling me in close so I could hear her whisper clearly.

"I'll see you in the morning, David."

"Looking forward to it."

She bit her lip, shutting the door behind me as I made it out into the cold hallway.

Seven o'clock sharp and I was sitting in the interrogation room. I barely had enough time to shoot Irina a text telling her I wasn't sure when I'd be out. I felt the beads of sweat trickle down the back of my neck wondering what they were going to hit me with. It wasn't like I didn't see this shit coming. I was sure there were many Playa Vista Towers residents who couldn't wait to tell the cops all about my behavior lately. They probably told them all about the fights Jade and I'd have at all hours of the night. I couldn't deny any of it, but no matter which way I looked at this shit, it wouldn't be hard for them to paint me as the guilty one.

"Good morning, Mr. Richardson. Thank you for coming down here so quickly."

"Anything I can do to help."

"We just wanted to ask you a few more questions about your wife's disappearance. You did say it was out of the ordinary for her to just vanish, like it wasn't something that she did often, but you were pretty clear that you two didn't have the best of a relationship," said the Detective.

"It's no secret that Jade and I had problems. We got married young, made a few reckless choices, and we weren't always happy, but I was content. I'm not so sure about her, but that doesn't matter now. All I want is for her to be home safe."

"I understand. I want you to walk me through what you were doing the night she disappeared, one more time. I just want to make sure we have all the details straightened out," he said.

I knew exactly what he was doing, trying to catch me in a lie so he could pin this shit on me. I took him through everything I could remember, shutting down every jab he tried to take, and it was like I could see them coming from a mile away. I wondered how long it was going to take them to turn the tables on me, painting me as the bad guy when they couldn't find the evidence that told them what really had happened to Jade. We had plenty of glass-shattering fights, the kind of bickering that made this shit look like an open and shut case.

Which angle are you going to take now, Detective Blanton? What version of the story are you trying to paint today? I sat there for what felt like hours, and when he finally shut his file, letting me know this shit was over, I sighed in relief. I made it back home, barely having a minute to myself before I got a knock on my front door. I opened it up to find Irina standing there clutching her Dior, staring at me blankly. I imagined she had a million thoughts running through her mind.

"I was worried about you," she said, stepping inside. I shut the door behind her, as her arms wrapped around my neck and pulled me in for a kiss. It felt good to feel her lips on mine after the last few days I'd had. I was already leading her towards the bedroom when she stopped me.

"There will be plenty of time for that, but first I need to know if you had anything to eat," she said, raising her eyebrow at me.

"Trust me, Irina, after the morning I had, I'm not hungry."

"Let me get you something, please?"

I didn't want to argue with her because the last thing I needed right about now was to be alone again. I was tired of having to deal with this shit, and she was right. If I didn't take the time to eat and calm down, I was going to lose my goddamn mind. She took out the leftovers I had in the fridge, put them in the microwave. As she was washing her hands, she glanced up at me.

"You know, David, we've been seeing each other for a while now, and I really feel quite close to you. I want you to know there isn't anything you could say that would ever scare me away," she said. She wiped her hands on the dish towel hanging on the oven door, patiently waiting for me to respond. I furrowed my eyebrow at her wondering what the hell she could even be getting at.

"Thank you, Irina," I said. I tried to shut the conversation down as fast as possible because I didn't need Irina breathing down my neck. All I wanted was to whisk her off to my bed and get lost between the sheets for the next few hours, but she seemed reluctant today, like she needed to get something off her chest first.

"What's bothering you?" I asked, noticing the change in her expression. She handed me the plate and a fork, but I couldn't take a damn bite until she spoke.

"I hate to ask you this, David, but I need to know. Did you have something to do with what happened to Jade? Look, I know you two have had your differences, and if you did, I'd just want to know," she said. My eyes widened and I got up, grabbed her by the arm, and led her right to the front door.

"Of all the people I expected to ask me that, you weren't one of them. I thought you knew me better than that, Irina."

"But, David. David, wait, I - "

I slammed the door in her face, staring at the empty, dirty apartment before me, wondering how the hell I let everything get so screwed up. *What the hell happened to you, Jade? If I don't find out soon, they're going to throw me in the slammer and our friends are going to be the ones to put me there.*

3

MIA

7 Days Missing

I haven't slept in days. I toss and turn, imagining where Jade could be. I wonder if she's hurt, if she's in pain, or worse. I'd been told by the cops many times that the first forty-eight hours are crucial, but we were nowhere close to finding out the truth then and we certainly aren't now. I turned around to see a sleeping Aaron laying next to me, clutching his pillow, and part of me wished I could be that calm. I carefully slid out of bed as soon as the sun started peeking in through our bedroom window.

I made my way to the kitchen, and started a pot of coffee. The aroma immediately jolted me awake. I caught sight of my cell phone sitting next to my laptop on the coffee table. I rushed over to pick it up, dialing the cops for an update. I had no choice but to be persistent, hoping that someone had heard something by now. It was eating me alive knowing that Jade could be out there somewhere fighting for her life and we'd have absolutely no idea. I tried to relax, listening to the phone ring until it connected.

"I'd like to speak to Detective Blanton," I said.

"What is this regarding?"

"The disappearance of Jade Richardson. I am calling to see if there's been an update in her case."

"Are you family?"

"You know, I'd really like it if you people would stop asking me that question. Jade is my best friend. She doesn't have a good relationship with her husband, and she doesn't talk to any of her immediate family. I care about her, and I want to bring her home safely. Please, can I talk to Detective Blanton?"

"He's busy at the moment, but if you leave your name, I can have him call you back," said the woman, sounding as disinterested as ever.

"My name is Mia. Detective Blanton knows who I am. He's heard my statement. Is there anything else you can tell me?"

"This is an ongoing investigation, Mia. Detective Blanton will reach out if he has any further questions. In the meantime, it's best you check with Jade's family for an update."

"But I just said - "

She hung up on me. I felt so frustrated I nearly chucked my phone halfway across the apartment, but the last thing I wanted to do was wake Aaron up too early again. He'd been such a sweetheart lately supporting and comforting me, but I was starting to worry it was taking a toll on our relationship. I poured myself that cup of coffee, standing in the doorway of our bedroom, smiling as he rubbed his eyes, looking back at me.

"What are you doing up so early?" he asked, groggily.

"I couldn't sleep again."

"Oh, Mia. Come here."

I set my piping hot coffee down on the nightstand, sliding back into bed with him, and he wrapped his arms tightly around me. We laid there for a while and I relaxed a little with how good it felt until his phone started vibrating, nearly falling off the nightstand before he caught it. He turned to kiss me softly before peeling the covers back and heading straight for the bathroom. I laid there wishing we could stay in bed all day again like we used to do every Sunday, but ever since Aaron had been so wrapped up in work, it was like I barely saw him.

A little while later I heard the shower turn off, and out he came with his towel tied around his waist. Beads of water dripped from his chest, slipping over his perfect six-pack abs, while he searched through his closet looking for the right suit for his upcoming meeting.

"I wish you didn't have to go today," I said.

"I'm sorry, Mia. I know things have been crazy lately, but I promise that once this deal gets approved, I'll be much more available. I hate to leave you worrying like this."

He got dressed quickly, running his fingers through his dark hair before taking a seat at the edge of the bed, caressing my cheek slightly.

"You have to get back to living your life, Mia. Jade wouldn't want you sitting around here wasting every hour of every day. I know it's hard to let go of this and let the police handle it, but that's the only option you have right now," he said.

I didn't say a word because I didn't want us to fight before he'd have to spend his day showing his investors around Playa Vista Towers. It was so strange for him to be so close yet so far all of the time. Even though I knew he would be just a few steps away, I couldn't help but feel as lonely as ever.

"I love you, Aaron."

"I love you too. I'll hopefully be home for dinner, but if things run late, I'll let you know."

I nodded, watching him grab his phone and his keys, rushing out through the front door. I sighed, pulling the covers up over my head, hoping that a little rest might do me some good. No matter how hard I tried, I just couldn't relax. I downed the cold coffee on the nightstand, made the bed, and decided to head down to the gym to work out. *Maybe I can lounge by the pool afterwards. I'm sure a little sun would do me some good right about now.*

I got into my gym clothes, and made my way across the courtyard when I saw Jordan heading in at the same time as me. He held the door open, smiling politely. We said a quick hello before I walked straight to the treadmill. Once I got my body moving again, I felt like I could truly think. It was somewhere between my increased incline and heightened speed that I realized I needed to be the one to start doing some digging of my own if I wanted to get any answers about what happened to Jade.

The cops are no help. The people around here love to gossip. I'm sure I can get something I can use out of them. Someone had to have seen Jade the night she disappeared. I have to find enough that will make the police have no choice but to listen. If they won't do something about it, I will.

~

I ordered myself a fruity cocktail, grabbed a book and my sun hat and went down to the pool hoping I'd be able to get out of my head for a little while. I laid out, feeling the afternoon sun on my skin. The warmth was truly refreshing.

"Here you are, miss," said the poolside waiter. He brought out my bright pink drink and set it down on the table next to me.

"Thank you." I took the drink in my hands, twirling the little pink umbrella, and that's when I turned my head to see who'd been sitting next to me.

"Laura?"

"Oh my God, Mia. It's so nice to see you. I feel like it's been forever. We missed you at Irina's dinner the other night," she said.

"Yes, well I didn't feel up to it with everything going on. It's been really hard on me."

"I know it has, dear. Have there been any updates?" she asked.

I knew that Laura was one of the only other people besides myself that actually cared enough to ask that question. She cared about Jade deeply, too. I wished I could tell her that the cops were on their way to figuring this out.

"I called the police this morning hoping to speak to the detective, but they denied me. Another spiel about how I'm not family and I should check with them instead. David is the last person I want to be asking anything, especially because part of me feels like he must be involved," I confessed.

I looked up at Laura who'd been staring at me blankly, twirling the straw in her drink as she tried to process what I'd just said.

"You really think he could be capable of doing something to hurt her? I know he isn't exactly a gentleman, and to be honest, he does treat Jade terribly, but I just can't imagine that he would go to such extreme lengths," said Laura.

"It's hard not to blame him after everything he put her through, but there is the possibility that he wasn't involved in this. I guess I'd rather blame him and feel like, if I do that, I have some answers than have none at all. I don't know what to do, Laura. I can't sleep. I can barely eat. Aaron keeps telling me I need to let this go for my own sake, but I can't. You understand that, right?"

"Oh, yes I do. Manny has been telling me the same thing. Ever since Jade went missing, I've been feeling uneasy. What if we have a hard core criminal living in our building? You know, Manny and I used to live downtown in a loft, but all of the sketchiness - well, that made it impossible to feel safe, so we moved here precisely because Playa Vista is known for its security bubble. We have guards at every entrance here. Security is out on bike patrols all day and all night, for goodness sake. How the hell did something like this happen here? I know that someone here knows something. I can just feel it, but I don't know who."

She sighed. I could see how exhausted she looked. *This really is keeping her up at night, too.*

"What do you think happened to her?" I asked. My mind ran wild with all the possibilities, and each made my stomach turn.

"I wish I knew. She was so excited about her YouTube channel taking off. She talked to me about all the plans she had and how she was going to be launching so much in the future, maybe her own branded products, she said, and that she was looking for investors. Now that we are called Silicon Beach, and Google and YouTube have moved into the neighborhood officially, it seems everyone and their mother has gotten 'first round funding'. Well, except for me! I wish I knew how everyone was tapping into this magical funding." Laura released her signature eye roll. "But anyway, yeah, I was really proud of her, and now this happens and I don't know what to think," said Laura.

"I had no idea it was that big. She talked about it a few times, and I promised her I'd never mention anything to David, but I didn't know she was looking for investors."

"She was ready to put her business on the map, and I told her to go for it. Sometimes I think that I'm responsible for all of this happening," said Laura.

"No, Laura. You can't blame yourself for this. I'm glad you were there for her. I'm glad we both were. I just wish I knew where to start looking for answers, because I feel like I keep hitting a wall."

"Ever since she disappeared, I've been going over the last time I saw Jade. I didn't pick up on it at first, but every time we spoke last week, she seemed distant. There was something clearly on her mind, something that made her jumpy, but I didn't think much of it at the time," said Laura, staring down at her fingers.

"Have you told the police this?"

"Gosh, yes. I've told them everything, but they just don't seem to have any leads."

"There has to be something that they're missing. I got the impression from the very beginning that they weren't exactly willing to go out on a limb here and really help. It seems like they're doing a terrible job on purpose, and that makes me worry that someone is blocking this investigation from actually happening," I confessed.

Laura stared at me blankly, shutting her eyes for a moment to take a deep breath. Her lips parted, ready to say something, but she stopped herself. I felt someone approach from behind, and when I turned I saw Manny standing there with a towel slung over his bare chest, ready to take the lounge chair next to Laura.

"Hello, Mia. It's good to see you."

"Hi, Manny. You, too. Well, I better be going now. It was nice chatting with you, Laura. We'll certainly do it again some time," I said, and she nodded.

I could see in her eyes that she understood this conversation was far from over, and now my mind was feeling much more confused than it had been before. *You were acting strange indeed, Jade. I thought you were anxious about your career or about dealing with David, but now I'm starting to think it was much more than that.*

I waited up for what felt like years, clutching the blanket to my chest on the couch, staring at the front door. I called Aaron a few times, but he didn't so much as text me that he was going to be late again. I looked over at the dining room table where the cold Thai takeout sat, and my state of worry started to kick into overdrive. *Where the hell is he? Why didn't he at least let me know he was going to be late?* I checked the time on my cell phone screen, realizing it was after one in the morning. My stomach started doing somersaults again.

I heard footsteps in the hallway, and I saw a shadow under the front door as the keys turned in the lock. I breathed a sigh of relief, but it didn't help the anger I felt flowing through me.

"Mia, what are you still doing up?"

I furrowed my brows at him, wondering how that could possibly be the first thing he asked me. I bit my lip for a moment, trying not to let my frustration get the best of me.

"I was waiting for you. If I remember correctly, we were supposed to have dinner together. You said you'd call or text if you were running late. Now, I can't imagine that your business meeting ran *this* late," I said, through my teeth.

"I'm sorry, Mia. I was with the board. We were at the bar, having a few drinks. I was trying to get the deal passed. I think I may have succeeded," he said, undoing his tie.

He sat down next to me, kissing me softly, but I pulled away. I felt his hands brush against my arm, trying to make things better, but I couldn't shake how mad I was.

"My best friend disappeared without a trace. The last bit of communication we had was a single text and I was supposed to meet her for brunch the next morning. I went to bed that night thinking nothing was going to happen, and now she's no longer here. You couldn't even send me a text to let me know you were alright. I don't care about the deal or how busy you were. You should understand that," I said, feeling the tears start to stream down my face.

I felt him caress my cheek as I shut my eyes, and he kissed my forehead.

"I'm so sorry, Mia. I didn't think about it like that. I love you, and I promise I won't let this happen again, okay?"

"I love you too. Thank you."

He grabbed my hand, leading me to the dining room so we could warm the takeout together. As we started pulling the food out of the delivery bag, his cell phone started to ring. I didn't get a chance to glance down at the screen to see who it was. I tried to brush it off, until he raced to pick it up.

"It's someone from the board. I have to take this," he said, kissing my head quickly before heading right out the front door.

What kind of call is so important you can't even have it in the apartment? I asked myself. I slowed my breathing and pressed my ear up against the door hoping I'd catch some of the conversation. He must have stepped far enough away because I couldn't hear a thing. *What are you up to, Aaron? What's gotten into you?*

4

LAURA

12 Days Missing

$\mathcal{I}$ put the kettle on to make myself a cup of tea to calm my nerves. I reached into the cabinet for a mug and a teabag, just as Manny came out yawning, looking rather tired. We both hadn't been getting much sleep these past few days. Every time I shut my eyes, all I could think about was Jade. It had been nearly two weeks since she went missing, and everyone seemed to go about their business as usual, but I just couldn't. The thought of where Jade might be and what she could be dealing with right now rattled me. It left me shaken, wishing that there was some way I could just relax, and that's when I decided it was time to get everyone back together again.

"Manny?"

"Yes, darling?" he asked, opening up the paper to peruse the news.

"How would you feel if we had everyone over for dinner tomorrow night? It's been a while since we were all together, and things were still quite awkward at Irina's a few weeks ago. I think it's time we all find a way to work through this instead of just ignoring each other, hoping this nightmare would just go away."

"Are you sure that's such a good idea, Laura? I mean, everyone's on edge, and rightfully so. We live in one of the safest complexes in the city and yet, Jade went missing. Maybe we need to give everyone their space."

"I think the last thing we all need right about now is space. Please?"

"Ah, alright," he said.

"Thank you, love. What would you like for breakfast?"

He smiled at me, putting the paper down on the breakfast nook, pulling me in for a kiss. I whipped out the frying pan to make him some French toast and eggs like we used to have at that little café in London on vacation. It was nice to sit down with him and enjoy our breakfast together before he'd head off for his morning walk around the complex. I had lots to do, making sure I called everyone to let them know they were invited, and a menu to plan that would knock everyone's socks off. *I think we could all use a bit of comfort food right about now. Maybe I should head over to Mia's to invite her personally. Something tells me she won't be too inclined to come over if she knows I'll be inviting David. I'm sure I can convince her, especially since I won't be taking no for an answer.*

Manny left in his running shorts and white t-shirt, clutching a water bottle to help beat the Los Angeles heat. I made my way to the shower so I could get ready for the day.

I clutched my woven tote bag to my side, my current novel of choice inside peeked out ever so slightly. My heeled sandals barely made any sound on the lush carpet as I walked down the high-ceilinged hallway, peering out the windows at the beautiful sunny day that was calling my name. I desperately wanted to head down to the beach, but I knew that if I wanted to throw together a perfect dinner tomorrow night, I'd have to start the preparation right away. *Groceries first, then I can relax a little.*

I took the elevator up to Mia's floor, wondering if she'd even be home. I knocked on her front door, and heard giggling coming from down the hall. A couple passed me with a smile, dressed like they were about to spend the entire day out by the pool, and before I could say hello to them, the door opened.

"Laura? What a nice surprise. Please, come in."

"Thank you, Mia."

I walked into her beautiful, luxe apartment space with her perfectly trendy beige couch, the candles lit on the glass coffee table, and the sound of her diffuser humming near the floor-to-ceiling windows. It was quite a step-up from the quaint unit I shared with Manny, but I was more than grateful to be living in such a beautiful place. It seemed rather dull ever since Jade went missing, like it lost its luster, and all I could do was hope that it would one day return. Mia looked absolutely beautiful with her deep brown eyes and silky black hair pulled back into a low ponytail.

She wore a pastel green sundress and a cream cardigan, settling into the armchair next to me so we could catch up.

"I hope I'm not keeping you, Mia."

"Nonsense. You know you're always welcome here," she said, with a smile.

Even though she smiled widely and her eyes were just as bright as ever, I could still tell that she was struggling with this just as much as I was. I was desperately looking for an escape, a chance to return to what life was like before Jade went missing. I was so sure dinner would do the trick. *At least, I hope it will.*

"Would you like something to drink? Maybe some tea?"

"No, that's quite alright. I'm actually here because I wanted to invite both you and Aaron to dinner tomorrow night. We've all been apart for so long and I plan to have everyone come. I know it's been a difficult time, but I miss that sense of community we had, you know?"

She cocked her head to the side, lowering her eyebrows as she looked at me, and I could already tell that she wasn't too excited about the idea.

"Will he be coming?"

"David?"

"Yes. I don't think I can look him in the eye or even say two words to him, Laura. I have this gut-feeling that he's somehow responsible for what happened to Jade and I don't know if I can let that go," said Mia.

"What's going to happen if you find out that he didn't have anything to do with it, Mia? I know how much it seems like he has to be involved, but I think we should at least give him the benefit of the doubt until there's more evidence. The fact is, we don't know the whole story right now. Even if you come, there's no obligation to speak to him. I just miss having everyone together, and I'm sure you do, too."

"I do."

"Do you remember when Jade would get us all to gather around at dinner and make sure that everyone had their favorite food to eat even if she had to make it herself?" I asked.

"She used to spend all day in the kitchen trying to make vegan chicken tenders for Nora. They never came out quite right, but Nora didn't care," Mia responded, with a chuckle.

"Those were some good times, weren't they?"

"You do know that we can have good times again, right?"

She pursed her lips, deep in thought about what to do, and that's when I caught her looking around her apartment. She'd been holed up in here for a long time, staying away from everyone, and I was sure she knew that she couldn't go on like this forever. She lifted her chin, taking a deep breath, and finally agreed to come.

"I'm so glad you said yes, Mia. Dinner is never the same without you, even when Aaron stops by in your place. I want you to remember how close we all were before Jade disappeared, and I'd like to think she'd want us all to be together right now. Don't you?"

"I suppose. She loves dinner parties, especially when you're the one cooking," said Mia, with a chuckle.

"I'll be making her favorite. Well, I'm off to Whole Foods to get what I need. I look forward to seeing you tomorrow night," I said.

"Let me know if you need any help tackling that beef Wellington," she responded. "Maybe you'll let me in on your top secret recipe."

"Ah, I will. Thank you, Mia."

I smiled warmly at her, as she held the door open. I could feel her watching me walk down the hallway to the elevator. On the ride down to the lobby, I thought about how terribly awkward tomorrow night could be. I shook my head and hoped that awkwardness would eventually dissipate and we'd all be comforted by the fact that we were together again. *We're all looking for answers, but I don't think we're going to find them if we keep avoiding each other. This dinner is an important step. It's a night out, a comforting event, we all need this so much right about now.*

It was a convenience to have such a big grocery store nestled into the Playa Vista Towers complex. Shopping there was a treat that almost replaced my love for Trader Joe's. I grabbed a basket at the entrance, glanced down at the little grocery list I'd written for myself, and decided where to begin. *I still have to call everyone and make sure they're available. Gosh, I probably should've done that before I started to shop.*

I started walking through the aisles, taking in the subtle scent of cinnamon sugar in the air. I was surprised to see that they were handing out samples at a time like this. The samples were boxed individually, sitting on the stand as people lined up to grab one. In that line, I spotted a familiar face.

"Brenda!"

She turned around. With a dimpled smile, she approached me clutching her basket.

"Laura, oh my God! It's so nice to see you!"

"You know, you are just the person I needed to see today."

"Oh, really? Now, whyever could that be?" she asked, teasingly.

"I'm having a dinner party tomorrow night and I wanted to get the word out to everyone because it has been such a long time since we all had some time together. After everything that happened, I miss the times when we'd all enjoy our evenings together and laugh. So, hoping to break some of the tension, I'm cooking," I said, with a chuckle.

"I can pass the word along to everyone for you. What time should we all swing by?"

"Seven o'clock should do just fine. Thank you, Brenda. It was something I should've done before coming down here to shop, but it completely slipped my mind," I confessed.

"Not a problem at all, Laura. Leave it to me. Everyone will be there."

I smiled as she took off to get her cinnamon sugar donut sample. At that moment, my stomach started to growl too. I got everything I needed, carried my bags back up to the apartment, and started thinking about what to make for lunch. I passed through the lobby, feeling the cool air conditioning hit me while I made my way to the elevator. I heard arguing coming from the other corner of the room and I turned around to see Irina standing there with her hand on her hip, pointing at Serge's face angrily.

It amazed me that the two of them were still together because I couldn't remember a time where they weren't fighting. I tried my best not to look because I didn't want Irina to rush over and try to make it seem like it wasn't as bad as it was. She was one of the only people in our friend group that I had a hard time getting along with. The mean, entitled behavior she exhibited every single day never failed to rub me the wrong way. I brushed it off, breathing a sigh of relief when I was finally alone in the elevator, enjoying the quiet ride up to my floor.

~

I set my wine glass down on the table outside on the balcony, turned on the lovely fairy lights, and took in the warm evening air. I heard the doorbell ring, and Manny yelled that he'd take care of it while I brought out all of the delicious, warm food. I placed serving spoons in each dish, and smiled at my beef Wellington because it came out perfectly. *I wish you were here to enjoy this, Jade,* I thought, heading back inside to meet each of the guests as they arrived.

Our guests funneled in and soon my entire apartment was filled with everyone in our friends' circle. We all enjoyed our drinks, catching up before it was time to finally sit down for dinner. It was already seven-thirty and the only person left to walk through my front door was Mia. I was about to ask Aaron where she was or if she was even coming when I heard a soft knock on my door.

"Mia, I'm so glad that you could make it," I said.

She cocked her head to the side, peeking in to see who had arrived, and when she saw David, her eyes widened. I watched as she took a deep breath, handing me a rather expensive bottle of wine, and I smiled.

"This is for you. I thought it would pair perfectly with the Wellington," she said.

"That is so thoughtful of you, Mia. Please, come in."

I called everyone to sit for dinner, glancing over at Mia who fidgeted and could barely sit still. Aaron reached over to hold her hand, and that seemed to calm her down.

"Thank you all for joining Manny and me here tonight. I know it's been a long time since we were all together, and I'm glad to see each and every one of you. I hope you enjoy the meal. Now, let's dig in," I said.

Everyone started passing the dishes around, the stories took off, the laughs ensued, and at that moment, we forgot about the terrible thing that happened to one of our own. I looked over at David who smiled as he got a piece of the Wellington and he glanced up at me, beaming.

"Oh, she would've loved this," he said.

The sadness returned to his eyes and I felt terrible, but I tried my best to keep the mood light so that we could all share the break we so desperately needed. The candles burned, the clanking of silverware on my china plates continued, and everyone seemed to be having a wonderful time. It wasn't long before my mind started to wander off, wondering where Jade was, and if she was alright. No matter how many times I tried to stop thinking about it, it would always come back.

The uncertainty was far too difficult to handle sometimes. In this moment, I felt comforted by everyone being here with me. I caught a glimpse of Mia across the table and it warmed my heart to see some of the hardness in her expression start to melt away. In our time as neighbors, I had come to think of Mia almost like one of my own daughters. *I guess this truly was the right move to make. Maybe now we'll get back to a point where we're involved in each other's lives again. It may help us cope until we find out the truth about where our Jade could be.*

Mia helped me clear the dishes from the table and I noticed that Manny held the front door open as everyone started leaving. David was the last to take off, and he seemed to look at Manny strangely, whispering something before making his way down the hallway. I raised an eyebrow at my husband, nearly dropping the dishes in my hand, but Mia managed to steady me and catch them right before they slipped.

"Everything okay, Laura?"

"Yes, I guess I'm just a little distracted is all," I said.

"I know the feeling well. I wanted to thank you for insisting that I come tonight. I thought I wouldn't be able to handle it or that I'd blow up on David again, but I didn't. It was refreshing to be around everyone, but - "

"It just made you miss her more, huh?"

"Yes, exactly. I don't know what's going on here or what happened, but if there's one thing I'm certain of, it's that Jade would've never just left without saying something. It's not who she is. She would never want us to worry like this. We were like family," Mia murmured.

"I know, hun. I know."

I saw her eyes glaze over like she was about to cry. She stopped herself at the last moment, inhaled sharply through her nose, shook her head slightly to clear the tears, and stood up a little straighter. She took the plates in her hands to the kitchen. It wasn't long before I was wrapping up leftovers for her, ready to tackle the mess and the trash before I turned in for the night. I handed her a tupperware container and she grinned.

"I can't wait to eat this tomorrow for lunch. Are you sure you don't want me to stay and help finish cleaning up?"

"No, no. It's perfectly alright. I can definitely take it from here. Have a lovely evening, Mia."

"You too, Laura. Thanks again."

I started on the dishes and got most of them done. By the time I was ready to take out the trash, I had no idea where Manny was.

"Manny?" I called out, but there was no answer.

I didn't think much of it, knowing that he has a tendency to fall asleep after he'd had too much wine. It was possible he was already in bed. I tied up the trash bags, and took them down the hall to toss down the chute. I slowed down as I approached the garbage room because I could've sworn I heard his voice nearby. I squinted, tugging on my bottom lip with my teeth. He was on the phone, loudly whispering with someone.

"I don't know what you want me to do, David. I don't know what I saw or if I even saw anything at all. What? What do you want from me?"

Manny sounded angry. I stood there in the hall with my trash bags in hand, my expression blank, waiting for him to see me. I watched his entire face change the moment he looked over at me, and he rushed to get David off the phone. I didn't say a word to him. I tossed the bags down the chute, and said nothing until we were both back inside.

I folded my arms across my chest. I turned to watch Manny lock the front door. He raised his eyebrows at me like he had no idea why I was even concerned.

"Manny, what was that all about?"

"It was just David acting up as usual. The man's been going through some shit lately. He's drunk all of the time. I'm surprised he didn't show up shitfaced tonight. He just needs some time to cool off."

"What did you see that makes him so concerned, Manny? Was it Jade?" I asked.

He sighed deeply, rolling his eyes, and shaking his head.

"Look, hun. I don't know what he's talking about, okay? Can you just let it go?"

I nodded, standing there shocked in the middle of our living room. I'd never seen him like that, but I settled on the fact that this could've just been a little too much for him. He used to be quite friendly with David before everything happened, and watching him spiral out of control was certainly starting to get to Manny. I took a deep breath, trying to calm myself down, and I decided it was time for a late-night cup of tea to ease my worry.

I heard the shower running while I sipped on a piping hot cup of chamomile, and a little while later, Manny came out in his fluffy robe. His expression was soft, slightly sad like he was upset with himself about yelling at me like that. He took me into his arms, kissing my forehead softly, before lowering his lips to my own. I melted into him like I did every time before, and he caressed my cheeks, whispering an apology in my ear.

"I'm sorry, Laur. I should've never taken my frustration out on you. It's just hard seeing David practically lose his mind, you know?"

"I know, darling. I understand."

~

The next morning, I was hoping to wake up feeling well-rested and refreshed after a nice dinner with my friends, but I didn't. I had been dreaming about Jade again, and after the little squabble with Manny last night, it only made me more curious. I wondered for a moment if Mia's suspicions had been right and there was something strange going on with David after all. I tried to shake it off, to go about my day as I would normally, but the more I thought about it, the more I began to worry it was true. *David always seemed so confused and lost, but certainly not dangerous. Maybe I don't know him as well as I think I do,* I thought.

I opened up the fridge looking for the milk when I realized there were extra tupperware containers in the fridge filled with leftovers.

"Manny? Who didn't take their leftovers last night?"

"I think it was David," he said, from behind his newspaper.

"I should take them over to him."

Manny looked up briefly, his lips parting like he wanted to object, but he settled back in, letting me go. I pulled my hair back into a low ponytail, grabbed the leftovers, and headed right out the front door. Part of me wanted to question Manny more about what happened, but after seeing the way he blew up last night, I didn't want it to happen all over again.

Maybe David will be more willing to talk. I thought. I couldn't help but wonder what I was walking into if David really was as dangerous as Mia made him out to be. I took a deep breath, walked down the hallway, and took the elevator to his floor. When I arrived at his apartment, I couldn't bring myself to knock on the door. I was about to turn right around to leave when I heard the lock move, and it was like I was frozen in my place. The door swung open like David was in a hurry, but he stopped the moment he saw me.

Seeing his gym t-shirt under his zip-up jacket and the shorts he was wearing told me he was off to work out. I felt terrible for interrupting, but he seemed glad to see me. There was a warm smile on his face, one I hadn't seen in a long time. It made me feel a bit better about how suspicious and doubtful I'd been.

"Laura, what brings you here?" he asked.

"I opened up my fridge today to find that you didn't take your leftovers home last night. I know you've been so busy lately, and I thought that they might help," I said.

"Yes, I'm sorry about that. I was in a bit of a rush to get back home last night to answer some urgent work emails. Thank you for bringing these over, Laura. Would you like to come in?"

He glanced behind him once, and I imagined that was because the place wasn't as clean or as organized as he'd like it to be, but I didn't mind. The warmth in his expression and that smile made me comfortable enough to head inside, even if I was about to ask him some rather uncomfortable questions.

"I have to say, Laura, I really didn't expect the invitation to dinner last night, but I'm grateful. It was nice to see everyone and not be questioned about Jade every minute. It was also nice to see her favorite meal there, too. Made me miss her a lot," he said.

"I'm glad you had a nice time, David. I thought it was time everyone got together. Ever since Jade disappeared, it's like we don't know each other anymore. Yesterday made me feel like we're still as close as we always were."

"Yes, well, I'm sure there are still a few of our friends that have reservations about me," he said, glancing down at his feet.

"They will come around. They're all just looking for answers and for someone to blame."

"I know, Laura. Thank you."

"I have to ask, David, I overheard some of the call you had with Manny last night. He didn't tell me much, but I just wanted to make sure you were okay."

"Y-Yes. I'm fine, Laura. Thank you. It's just, things have been quite difficult and I'm also trying to find out the truth here. I've gone over every detail I could remember of the night she disappeared, but I still can't figure it out. To be honest with you, I was drunk for most of it. Now, I'm stuck with this nightmare. I just don't know what to do," he said.

"Walk me through it. Maybe I can help."

He looked at me gratefully, but I could still see the bit of nervousness behind his eyes like he was afraid to tell me just how bad things really were. He shuffled around in his seat, fixing the cushion behind him a few times, until he finally took a deep breath.

"We were fighting because Jade accused me of sleeping around. I told her that I'd never do that to her, but she didn't believe me. I was drunk, too drunk to do anything other than yell at her, but I'd take it all back if I could. She was trying to tell me something, but I didn't listen. I've been trying to figure out if she was going to tell me that she was in some kind of trouble or someone was trying to hurt her, because I knew she wouldn't just leave. She may have left without telling me, but she wouldn't leave without telling Mia or you."

I wasn't sure if it was the frustration that was getting to him or the fact that the police were probably on his tail trying to prove whether he hurt Jade or not, but his eyes filled with tears. I stayed with him, listening to him tell me every little detail he could remember about the nights leading up to her disappearance. I sat there wondering if it was all connected somehow.

I still can't be completely sure that he's innocent, but now I know Jade was hiding something. I wonder if she shared that with Mia. I need to talk to her about it, or maybe I shouldn't. Maybe it's not my place. I thought, getting ready to leave, realizing I now had more questions than answers.

"Thank you for stopping by, Laura. I know this goes without saying, but can you please keep this conversation between us?"

"Of course, David. I'll see you around. Enjoy your leftovers," I told him, pointing at the fridge.

"I will."

5

MIA

30 Days Missing

I was sitting alone at one of the Playa Vista Towers restaurants for brunch. My cell phone started ringing so I took it out of my purse and saw that it was Laura. I hadn't seen her much these past few weeks since the dinner she hosted, but I imagined she was keeping herself busy. As much as we wanted things to remain the same, it grew harder for me to connect with the others. I didn't want to go to fancy dinner parties, spend my days shopping, or work on achieving my dreams knowing that Jade could be out there somewhere suffering. It took every ounce of effort to drag myself out of the apartment to eat something that hadn't been sitting in my fridge for the last few weeks.

"Hello?"

"Mia, I hope I'm not bothering you," she said.

"Not at all. I'm actually down by the Pearl Lounge for brunch. Would you like to join me?" I asked, realizing I was craving company more than I thought.

"Ah, yes, actually I'm walking across the courtyard now. I'll be there in a bit."

"Great. See you!"

I tucked the novel I was reading back into my purse, ordering myself another mimosa while I waited for Laura to arrive. I sat there wondering how an entire month could've gone by and there was still no news about Jade's whereabouts. I was sure that the police would at least have had a lead by now, but nothing had trickled down through the building gossip. *It's not like they'd tell me anything if I called and asked anyway. They've taken every opportunity possible to shut me down. It's not like I'm going to pick up the phone and call David either,* I thought, cutting into my fluffy pancakes as I spotted Laura. I waved at her, and she came over, followed by a waiter with a menu in hand. She thanked him kindly, then turned to me with a smile.

"It's been far too long since we've seen each other, hasn't it?"

"It has. I'm sorry I haven't called. I'm having a much more difficult time readjusting to life as normal without Jade it seems," I confessed. Normally, we would play tennis at least one afternoon every week, and we usually walked up to Starbucks several mornings without fail. Everything felt lonely and pointless now.

"I understand that. Mia, there's something I've been wanting to talk to you about. At first, I didn't think there was anything to it, but like you, I haven't been able to stop thinking about Jade, either. The night after my dinner, I spoke to David. He walked me through what he remembered from that night, and he made it pretty clear that Jade was hiding something from him. I just don't know what it could be."

"Why didn't you tell me about this sooner, Laura?"

"I just thought that maybe David was reading too much into things, but if he can barely remember that night and they were fighting so often, maybe he really is involved somehow," she said.

She could barely look me in the eye and she was toying

with her wedding band, probably hoping to cut the nervousness she was feeling, but it didn't seem to help much. I put my knife and fork down, took a sip of my drink, nodded as I listened to the rest of what she had to say. The Los Angeles sun beat down on us both. Brunch on the patio was usually a time to relax, but we were both even more on edge now that we were sure there was more to the story here.

"Did Jade tell you about anything that may have made her feel unsafe? Maybe someone that made her feel uneasy? I know she was in the middle of getting her business off the ground and all, looking for investors the moment it took off, but that could have been anyone that lives here," said Laura.

"I'm starting to think that she wasn't as open to talking as I thought she was. I had no idea that she was even expanding her business, remember? Some friend I am."

"I guess she wanted to wait until she found the right investor. Maybe she was waiting to share some good news for a change instead of telling you more about how difficult things were in her marriage. David did say that they were fighting about his infidelity the night she disappeared," Laura reminded me.

"Did he say that he did it?"

"He said that he'd never do that to her, but I don't believe him. The look in his eyes told me otherwise," she said.

"Who do you think it could be?"

"Who knows? It could be anyone. It could be a total stranger."

We finished up our meal and the waiter brought over our bill as I reached into my purse for my credit card.

"No, Laura, please I got it," I said.

"Let me at least pay for my coffee."

"Nonsense, it's on me. You didn't even eat anything," I murmured.

I paid the bill, and just as we were about to leave, I spotted Manny walking out of the gym with Jordan close behind him. I remembered what Laura had said about that strange phone call he shared with David, and I decided that it was time to ask him about it myself.

"What are your plans for the rest of the day?" I asked Laura.

"I'll probably be by the pool for a while and then I'll be baking up a storm most likely. Manny is having drinks with a friend this evening so I have the place to myself. You're welcome to come if you'd like."

"Thank you, Laura but I'm afraid I have plans tonight. Another time, though."

"Of course."

I watched as she walked off, waving to her husband before heading straight for the pool. I sighed, glancing down at my phone screen, realizing that I was late to meet Didi. *Shit. She's going to kill me,* I thought, grabbing my things, heading straight for the lobby.

I walked down the long, bright hallway to Didi's apartment, hearing the sound of boxes being tossed and thrown as I got closer. The expensive carpet beneath my feet muffled any sound I made and when I arrived at Didi's open doorway, I startled her.

"Oh my God. Mia," she said, catching her breath.

"I'm sorry, Didi. Looks like you're pretty wrapped up here, huh?"

Her blonde hair was freshly blown out, laying right above her chest in bouncy curls that moved with her while she packed old furniture pieces into the remaining boxes. Her bright blue eyes blinked at me and she tilted her head to let me know exactly where we needed to begin.

"I was hoping you'd be here a little while ago, but now that you are, we can start loading these in the service elevator."

"Is someone picking them up?"

"Yes, and taking them straight to my mother's. That woman is in desperate need of a furniture upgrade. She's been holding onto that awful deep mahogany furniture for a little too long," said Didi.

She was working up a sweat in her pants suit, and I made my way inside her apartment to get started on packing just as I promised. I noticed there was a neatly stacked pack of business cards that were sitting in an open box on a bed of tissue paper. I inched closer to it, taking them into my hands, my fingers brushing up against the gold embossed letters.

"Beautiful, aren't they?"

"Who did these for you?" I asked, knowing Didi was quite particular with the designers she hired.

She was one of the best realtors Los Angeles had to offer, and I knew there wasn't a deal she couldn't close or a house she couldn't sell when she put her mind to it. *She's the reason I'm even living here.*

"Surprisingly, not a designer with a long list of qualifications. I went with our lovely Jade instead. She really helped me rework everything. Before she disappeared, she was in the process of redoing my entire branding. She's really got a knack for what's trendy, being an influencer and all. It still shocks me that David didn't know how popular she was getting."

"David never really paid attention to anything she did, but that didn't stop her from finding happiness in her career," I said.

"Do you remember when we threw that ridiculous party for Brenda's birthday and everyone was coming up to her asking for pictures? One of them even asked for Jade to redo their entire closet. She always knew what to wear, who the best labels are, and what next to buy. I miss that."

"I miss that, too. Do you also remember what happened to her thousand dollar dress that night?"

"One of the waiters spilled wine all over her!"

"And she laughed it off, deciding to take a picture in her wine-stained dress," I said, with a giggle. "I think she got another thousand followers after posting that pic alone. She's a genius."

"God, I miss her."

"I miss her, too."

"I'm glad I decided to go with her. I decided to hold off until she finds her way home. I don't want to give the opportunity to anyone else," Didi murmured.

I smiled, knowing that would've made Jade so happy. *There are so many of us that believe in you, Jade. We all love you. All we want is to know what happened.* I thought, finding myself missing her a little more than usual today.

I tried to shake it off for the time being, sticking pieces of furniture and loose nails into boxes, taping them up, and carrying them out to the service elevator. I was surprised that Didi was practically getting rid of half of her apartment, but I knew just how often she liked to change things. *I'm starting to think that we're all in desperate need of a change right about now.*

We took a break for a moment and I sat at Didi's lavish breakfast bar while she slid a bottle of water to me across the marble countertop. It was cold, refreshing, and exactly what I needed. I drank it all in one go, and I looked back to see Didi rummaging around on the console table near the entryway.

"Ah, here it is," she said.

She brought over what looked like a black portfolio, and slid it over to me. I glanced up at her, furrowing my brow.

"What's this?"

"That's Jade's portfolio. She left it with me when I was deciding whether I was going to hire her to do my rebrand and, boy, did she blow me away. I thought it'd be best that you have it because I'm going on a work trip soon. You're going to see her before I do anyway," said Didi.

"Thank you."

I flipped through it, my fingertips brushing against each laminated page as I thought of all the time it must've taken Jade to put this together. It only made me miss her more, but it felt good to have a piece of her I hadn't seen much before. Part of me wished I would've spent more time listening to her when she went on about her job. I was far too concerned with what was happening in her marriage than to be happy for her because I was scared something bad might happen. *And it did. David has to be involved, right?*

"Didi, what do you think happened to Jade? Honestly?" I asked, the words tumbling out of my mouth fast.

She stopped in her tracks, looking back at me like she had absolutely no idea what to say, but I could practically see the thoughts flitting around behind her blue eyes.

"I think that husband of hers is to blame, if I'm honest. He's always given me the creeps and now he's been lurking around in corners with the police, pretending like he gives a shit about what happened to his wife. I say the husband did it," Didi said, straight to the point.

She was never one to sugarcoat anything. I sat there with my eyebrows raised, realizing that David really could've had a hand in all of this. *If you're the reason my best friend is missing, I will make sure you rot in jail. That's a promise.* I knew I needed to talk to Manny about what David told him, because even though Laura came to me herself, I still think he might've been hiding something from her.

"Laura and I seem to be on the same page with you there, Didi. He seems like the kind of guy to do something like this, but my question is why."

"He probably snapped. Those two fought a lot and about everything you could possibly imagine. Let's just hope he comes clean or the cops find something soon. All I want is to see Jade home safe."

"We all do, Didi. We all do."

~

I thumbed through the portfolio on my kitchen counter, studying all of Jade's work closely, when I realized there was some opened mail tucked into the back. They were a few client testimonials that were mailed in and I read them, knowing how much Jade loved her job. *Her clients seem to love her,* I thought, turning the letters around to see that the address on the front wasn't the one for her apartment with David. I wrinkled my brows, wondering what could be in apartment 206. *She never told me she had another space in the building. Is that where she's been working from all this time?*

I glanced over at the floor-to-ceiling windows in my apartment to see that the sun was starting to set now. I pulled out my cell phone, dialing Manny's number, hoping he wasn't going to screen my calls. There were a few people who'd been steering clear of me ever since I blew up on David in the middle of the lobby. I imagined Manny might've been one of them, especially because he apparently knew more than he was letting on, or at least that was what I hoped.

"Manny?"

"Mia? Hello. How are you?"

"I'm doing well. I wanted to know if there was any way we could meet. I know you're probably busy and have some plans this evening, but I'd love it if we could have a chat," I said.

There was a long pause before he answered, and I wondered whether he was going to try to get me to talk to Laura instead. Manny was always the kind of man that took a backseat to any problems and I knew how much he hated confrontation, but I wasn't about to take no for an answer. I felt an overwhelming responsibility to put the pieces together about what happened to Jade, and I wasn't going to let anything stand in my way.

"I, uh, I have dinner plans tonight, but I suppose you can swing by the rooftop lounge before that," he said.

"Great. I'll see you then."

That evening I tousled my soft natural curls, painting a light wash of pink over my lips before I grabbed my coat to head up to the rooftop lounge. My heart was beating fast in anticipation of what Manny would tell me if he'd be willing to tell me anything at all. I brushed the few wrinkles out of my satiny maxi dress, getting ready to head out the door when I heard it open.

"Aaron?"

"Hello, love. Where are you off to?" he asked, inquisitively, studying my appearance.

He smiled brightly and it warmed my heart to see him because we hadn't been spending as much time together as I'd like. I felt his arms wrap around me and his hand lifted my chin so he could press his lips to mine.

"I missed you," I said.

"I missed you, too. I always do."

He kissed me again, and for a moment I'd completely forgotten what I was about to do. All the tension that had settled between us was starting to melt away, and part of me wished I could spend the rest of my evening with him, but I knew that I couldn't.

"I should get going. I'm actually on my way up to the rooftop lounge to meet with Manny. He has some information about David and Jade. I know you told me that I need to let the cops handle this, but I just can't sit around anymore. There's no harm in asking a few questions, right?" I asked.

I was waiting to see if he was going to jump down my throat about it again, but he didn't. He simply smiled and nodded as he ran his fingers through my hair.

"Would you like me to come with you? I can, you know."

It was sweet of him, and it made me happy to know that even after all this time he was still supporting me through this.

"It's alright, Aaron. Thank you. When I get back, we can throw on a movie and eat something. I love you," I said, planting a soft kiss on his lips.

"I love you, too."

I took the elevator up to the rooftop lounge, and the evening air hit me like a tidal wave, with its cool breeze whipping my hair around. I caught sight of Manny sitting in one of his signature polo shirts, a gold chain around his neck, stirring his drink nervously like he absolutely did not want to be there. I headed in his direction, but before I could make it over to him, someone tapped me on the shoulder.

"Mia! Oh my God. I'm so glad to see you out and about. Everyone's been wondering what you've been up to lately. I know you've been dealing with a lot."

"Hello, Karen."

"Would you like to grab a drink with me? I'm actually supposed to be meeting a few friends and I - "

"I'm sorry, Karen but I'm actually here to talk to Manny. I'm sure we'll catch up some other time, okay?"

"Yeah, sure. Fine. Go drink with the old guy," she scoffed, heading back to her little fire pit booth.

I took a deep breath, sliding into the seat next to Manny, and his eyes widened like I scared him. I smiled warmly, trying not to jump down his throat too quickly about why I actually wanted to meet with him.

"Hello, Mia," he said, taking a sip of his bourbon.

"Hi, Manny."

"What did you want to talk about?"

"I wanted to ask you about that phone call you shared with David and about the night Jade disappeared. I think we both know there's a little more to the story than what Laura told me. So, please, don't leave anything out."

6

MANNY

30 Days Missing

*W*hat the hell does she want? I downed my drink while the bartender rushed over to top me off. Mia ordered herself something pink and fruity-looking while she waited for me to spill all the shit I knew. I wanted to turn on my heel and run, leave Laura to deal with this, but I knew that wasn't going to work anymore. *Why did she even tell Mia about the phone call? How involved do the two of them think I am?* I asked myself, adjusting the collar of my pale blue polo, watching as Mia stirred in the seat next to me.

"I don't know what you want me to say, Mia," I said, glancing down at my watch, knowing I was going to be late.

I had to meet Jordan because I promised him some sound medical advice in exchange for a steak dinner, but it didn't look like Mia was going to let me go until I told her something. *Do I really want to air David's dirty laundry? I mean, he really did bring this upon himself. Who knows? Maybe he's guilty after all.*

"I want you to tell me what David told you over the phone on the night of Laura's dinner party," she clarified.

"David's been on a bender lately. He's been drinking way

too much and he tends to blab a whole lot of nonsense. He's aware that I know that he fought with Jade the night she disappeared, and he didn't want me to say anything to anyone," I said.

"Why?"

"Why do you think, Mia? There's not a person in this entire building that doesn't suspect him. Everyone, including you, seems to think he has something to do with this."

"And you don't?"

"I don't want to blame the man until I know for sure. There is no evidence. David may not be perfect, and he's got a temper, and he has hurt her, but enough to cause all this commotion? He did love her a lot at one point. Yeah, maybe their marriage was over, but David wouldn't have just gotten rid of her."

"That's not enough for me. He's drunk half the time. He doesn't even remember what he has for breakfast and it amazes me that he's still able to keep his job. He could have snapped. He could've lost it for a split second and something terrible could've happened to Jade. Look, Manny, I feel like I'm going a little crazy here. Everyone wants to move on, but I won't be able to do that until I know what happened. You understand that, don't you?"

"I do, Mia. I know this is tough."

"So, tell me what else you know. He couldn't have been that upset because he didn't want you to tell anyone they fought that night. There has to be more," she said, and she was absolutely right.

There was definitely more, but I wasn't sure what was going to happen when I shared it. Mia was a strong-willed woman, but I was afraid that once she learned how on-edge Jade was leading up to her disappearance, she may suffer a similar fate. *Something terrible did happen here, Mia. I can practically feel it, but how am I going to live with myself if something happens to you, too? Someone out there knows what happened, and something tells me they're going to do whatever it takes to stop it from getting out.*

"I saw Jade that night," I murmured, and her eyes widened.

All of the memories came flooding back in an instant. It was just a brief second, riding down the elevator together, but if I had known that she'd really been in trouble, I would've done something. I thought about her beige duster coat, the light-wash blue jeans, and her chestnut brown hair pulled back into a low bun. I remembered the expression on her face, the fear in her eyes, and not a day goes by where I didn't wish that I said something to her. I told Mia about it, watching her clutch her drink so hard I thought she was about to break the glass.

"Laura mentioned that she seemed off the few days leading up to her disappearance. Is this true?"

"Very true. In fact, a few days prior, at around two in the morning, there was a knock on my front door. Laura was fast asleep and I answered it to find Jade standing there with an awful gash in her leg. The shape made it look like it was from the top half of a broken beer bottle. I helped clean it out and patch it up, offering to call the police, but she insisted it was just an accident."

"Did David do that to her?"

"That's what I'm guessing."

"You know that and you can still vouch for him?" asked Mia.

"It just doesn't make sense, Mia. The cops would have found something when they swept his place. There would've been indication of a struggle, something. If he was that drunk that night, how would he have been able to clean himself up? Yes, he's got his problems, but don't we all?"

"Not like that, Manny. We don't just go driving beer bottles into people when we're upset," she said, with her arms folded.

"You're right. You know, maybe he did have something to do with it, but my gut is saying no. Should she have left him a long time ago, sure, but something still feels missing here. She wasn't heading home when she was that afraid the last night anyone saw her. She wasn't afraid of heading home to David. She was afraid of someone else."

Mia nodded, and we talked for a little while longer about how difficult this had all been. I could tell that she was on the verge of losing her mind hoping there'd be answers somewhere, and part of me wished I could've given them to her. I bid her goodbye, just as Jordan came barreling through the door to the lounge so we could have dinner.

~

I slipped into a pair of basketball shorts and a white t-shirt to head down to the gym when I heard the shower shut off. Laura came out in a robe with her wet hair dripping on the carpet, and I made my way over to kiss her soft, supple skin. She smiled at me, and we were finally getting back to a place where we didn't have to fight anymore. I came clean to her about what I'd told Mia, about everything I'd bottled up inside for such a long time, and even at our age, it brought us closer.

"You're heading to the gym already? You haven't even had breakfast," she said, disappointedly.

"I promise I'll eat when I return. Just going for some light cardio," I responded, kissing her softly.

"Oh, alright."

I rode the elevator down to the lobby that seemed to be busier than usual today. I glanced outside the automatic doors to find a few police cars parked out front. Two of them stood huddled by the entrance, speaking something into their radios, but they stopped once they saw me. I was about to head in the opposite direction so I could make it across the courtyard to the gym when one of them approached me.

"Emmanuel Clark?" he asked.

"Yes, how do you know that?"

The look on his face frightened me, and I wondered why he

was studying me so closely like he expected I had something to hide. He lifted his cap and ran his fingers over his buzz cut hair, raising his eyebrows at me.

"Your friend, David, pointed you out in a group photo. He made a case about you being one of the last ones to see Jade alive. I'm going to have to ask you to come down to the station and answer a few questions," he said.

You son of a bitch. They were probably looking into you so you just had to point the finger at me, I thought, hoping to plead with the officer that they wouldn't get anything out of interrogating me, but before I could, I heard a familiar voice from behind me.

"What's going on here?" asked Aaron.

He looked like he just returned from the gym, sweat covering the neck of his t-shirt, dripping from his hair, and he had a water bottle in his hand he was probably guzzling moments before.

"I'm just trying to get Emmanuel here to cooperate. I wouldn't want to have to force you to come down to the station, but if that's the route you want to take, so be it."

"I-I'll be fine, Aaron. Thank you though. I'll meet you at the station, officer."

"Good. See you there."

He walked off, clutching a notepad to his side, and I could've sworn I saw a smirk on his face like he was getting a real kick out of all of this. I sighed deeply and Aaron turned to face me.

"Does Laura know?"

"That David practically told the cops I could have something to do with what happened to his wife? No, but I will have to eventually. I need to head back to the apartment to grab my car keys," I told him.

"Nonsense. Let me drive you. At least that way I can be sure they don't try to fuck you over."

"Are you sure, Aaron?"

"Yes, Manny. Look, we all need a friend in our corner, especially right now."

"Thanks, man."

"Don't mention it."

Why is David doing this? Why now? He's been sitting on this for so long and now he chooses to tell the authorities? He's covering his ass. Maybe Mia was right. Maybe he really did do this. The thoughts were swimming around inside my mind as Aaron drove me down to the police station. Aaron was a good guy to know, and he had political connections, so if worse came to worst, maybe he could call in a favor. He certainly could afford to post my bail if he were so inclined. I was nervous as hell, not going to lie. It was also the first time I had left Playa Vista Towers in ages, and I couldn't say I was excited to be out. I knew that Laura and I were practically living in a bubble, but I felt safe there. I felt like I could finally enjoy my retirement without any worry creeping up when I least expected it. *I was sure as hell wrong about that one.*

I felt comforted knowing that Aaron was right outside because at least I didn't have to deal with this shit alone. I glanced up at the fluorescent lighting over my head. A chill prickled down the back of my spine in the cold interrogation room. It felt like ages before the detective finally came waltzing in with a file in his hand.

"Emmanuel. Thank you for coming down. My name is Detective Blanton and I'd like to ask you a few questions about your missing friend."

"Your officer didn't give me much of a choice in the matter. I'm happy to help in any way I can to give you what you need to find Jade, but I don't appreciate what's going on here."

"And what is that exactly?" he asked.

"I'm sure you've questioned David countless times by now,

so I'd like to know why he had to bring me into this. Yes, I saw Jade the night she disappeared. We were riding the elevator together. I'm not sure if you're aware, but we live in the same goddamn building," I spat.

The nervousness made my legs shake and I felt a bead of sweat trickle down the back of my neck while Detective Blanton stared at me blankly. He didn't seem surprised or even taken aback by what I said, and that's when I wondered if he'd already made up his mind about what he thought happened to Jade. The rest of the interrogation went smoothly, so much so that when I was finally let out of the room, it didn't even dawn on me that it was over.

He doesn't think I did it. You tried to throw my ass under the bus here, David, but it didn't work. They've still got their eyes on you, and for good reason. You're one dangerous piece of shit.

"How did it go?" asked Aaron, leaning on the side of the building, waiting for me.

"It wasn't bad actually. Detective Blanton doesn't seem to be that interested in me after all. I still have to find out why David even told them about me in the first place. It could've gone a whole lot worse if he was gunning for someone else to blame."

"David's probably just running scared right now. The police have every right to look into what he's been doing, especially because of how he treated Jade. I know today didn't exactly go as planned and you were probably hoping to have a quiet morning at the gym, but I'm meeting with a few business associates tonight, and I'd like it if you'd joined me," said Aaron.

"That's nice of you to offer, Aaron, but I have to ask, why? I'm just an old, retired doctor and I'm not sure I'll have much in common with your business friends."

"Two of them are doctors and I'm sure you'll impress them. Besides, there will be an open bar. We could all use a drink right about now. I wonder how long it'll be before they start dragging us all down here to ask questions," he said.

"Well, if they do I'm sure it won't be that bad. It's not like you have anything to hide," I teased.

"Nope, but someone that we know probably does."

"All bets are on David. If he didn't have anything to do with Jade's disappearance, I'd be really surprised. I don't know any other sick fuck that would hurt someone so nice."

"They'll catch the right guy soon enough. All we can hope for is that we get to see Jade again, alive and well."

"Yeah, you're absolutely right."

Aaron took me back home, and from the moment I entered the lobby, I heard Laura call out my name. I glanced back at Aaron who just shrugged at me.

"I had to tell Mia who couldn't help but tell Laura. I'm sorry."

"No, no. You did the right thing. Thank you again, Aaron."

"No problem. I'll see you tonight," he responded, tapping me on the shoulder. I watched as he headed straight for the elevators just as Laura came barreling towards me. She wrapped her arms around me, squeezing tightly, and I could imagine how worried she'd been. I held her face, kissing her hard, and I could feel her breathe a sigh of relief.

"Oh my God, Manny. Are you okay? How did it go?"

"It was fine, Laur. They didn't seem too interested in me or what I had to say. Looks like they're still just trying to put the pieces together."

"Why did they call you down in the first place?" she asked, with a confused expression on her face.

"Let's talk about that later, shall we?"

We both glanced around to see that everyone was staring at us, and on our way back up, the cops came out of the elevator without saying a word to us. Once we were back in our apartment, Laura folded her arms across her chest, tossing her light brown hair over her shoulders, and waited for me to fill her in on what was going on.

"It was David."

"What do you mean it was David?"

"He's the one that went to the police and told them that I was one of the last people to see Jade alive. Coming from his mouth, that must've made them real suspicious," I said.

"Why the hell would he do that?"

"Because they're probably building a case against him and he's looking for a way out. On the bright side, Detective Blanton didn't pressure me or badger me with questions. I told him what I knew and he let me out. He didn't seem too interested in my story anyway."

"Well, that's a relief. I still don't understand why David would do that after everything we've done for him."

"He seems like he's at that point where he'll do anything not to end up in jail. It's probably best that we all stay away from him."

I was expecting Laura to fight me on this because all she wanted was for us to come together again and be as close as we once were, but she just nodded.

"I suppose you're right, dear. Until our dear Jade is home, I won't be spending any more time with David."

"It's for the best, love," I told her.

"I know it is."

I kissed her softly on the forehead, and went to take a shower while she fixed me something to eat.

I straightened my tie, brushing the few wrinkles out of my suit jacket while I took the elevator down to the lobby so I could walk to *The Vine*. It felt good to get out the house and talk to a few people from my old profession for a change especially after the day I've had. *I also can't argue with an open bar.* It wasn't until I got there that I realized Aaron had rented out the entire place for us. I found him standing with the four other guests he had with him, and he smiled the moment he locked eyes with me.

"Ah, Manny. Please, let me introduce you to everyone."

"Hello."

"This is Jack, Eric, Nick, and Brandon. Nick and Brandon here are the ones you're going to want to talk to. They're both neurosurgeons," he said.

I smiled, feeling an immense weight being lifted off my shoulders as I settled into the evening. I was surprised to see that Aaron would need so much privacy for such a small dinner, and that's when I realized there was more to this little get-together than just a night out.

"So, Aaron, I hope that you have good news for us. I know your last investment fell through, but we're ready to throw some money at whatever you think will be most profitable," said Jack. He looked over at me with a cold smile, and his graying hair fell into his eyes before he brushed it away. *This means business, doesn't it? Well, I'm sure Aaron's got this under control. He's been doing real well for himself lately,* I thought.

7

MIA

45 Days Missing

$\mathcal{T}$he sun poured into the apartment, beaming on the brass accents on the shelves. The coffee table books were neatly stacked in front of me, and I sat on the chaise lounge in my silk robe, recovering from yet another sleepless night. I dreamt of what Jade must be going through right now, and there were times I'd force myself to believe that she was happy wherever she was, even though my gut told me another truth. I sighed, lost in thought, but I was quickly jolted out of it by the incessant ringing of my cell phone.

"Hello?" I didn't even check the caller ID. When I heard the voice, it was shrill and full of excitement.

"Mia! Oh gosh, I hope I didn't wake you!"

"Not at all, Karen. How have you been?"

"Not good. Do you notice that everyone's been a little too hush hush about this whole Jade thing? Crazy isn't it? One minute you're here and the next... poof! God, I wish I knew what happened to her," said Karen. I heard the sound of silverware clinking and I imagined herself down at the restaurant having brunch like she did every Saturday morning.

"You and me both, Karen."

"Mia? Um, have there been any updates about Jade yet? I heard the cops were looking into David and I even heard they took Manny down to the station, too! I, uh, just wanted to know," she said.

The worry in her voice was unsettling, like there was something she wanted to say, but couldn't. Suddenly I felt a wave of uncertainty overcome me, making me as curious as Karen seemed to be.

"There haven't been any updates yet, as far as I know, Karen," I murmured.

"Are you sure? The police have to have some kind of lead by now, right? Are you sure they're even really doing everything they can?"

Her question took me by surprise and the hesitation in her voice seemed to grow with every passing minute.

"Wait a minute, Karen. Why are you asking me this?"

"I-I don't know. This whole thing's got me real messed up, Mia."

"Listen, give me a half hour and I'll come down. We can chat then."

I waited for a moment to see if she'd decline, but she didn't.

"Thank you, Mia."

Karen wasn't the kind of woman that ever wanted anyone to know how or what she was feeling. She pranced around like everything was perfectly fine when it wasn't, tearing into anyone that would get in her way. Hearing how scared she sounded only made me feel like there was something she wasn't telling me, and I was growing tired of feeling like I was being kept in the dark. *If it's something that will help me find you, Jade, then I have to know. I have to do whatever I can to bring you home.*

I hopped in the shower, the steam blanketing the entire bathroom as I quickly washed my hair. When I stepped out, tying a towel around my body, I realized just how tired I looked. I did my makeup swiftly, covering the dark circles under my eyes and the dullness in my skin. I pulled my wet, curly black hair back into a top bun, added some Mixed Chicks styling cream and went to my closet to pick out something to wear. I spotted a blouse hanging in my large walk-in closet. I hadn't worn it ever since Jade disappeared because she was the last one to wear it. I was drawn to its emerald green color, and I decided that today was the day.

I was dressed and ready to leave my empty apartment, wondering for a moment what Aaron was getting up to today. I vaguely remembered the soft kiss on my forehead before he left while I was still half asleep, but I missed him a little more than usual. *All business, all the time,* I thought, shaking off my frustration as I locked my apartment door behind me.

"Thank you for coming over," said Karen.

I spotted the single wine glass on the coffee table with what looked like the remnants of last night's Chardonnay still left in it. She cleared it away, asking me if I'd like something to drink. I shook my head, knowing that the tea I had earlier was still churning in my stomach because of how anxious I'd been.

"Of course, Karen. You sounded so distraught on the phone, I didn't realize this was affecting you this much."

"Everyone seems to think that just going on with our lives is the only way to go, but I can't. I'm afraid the cops are going to come knocking on my door to take me away in handcuffs," she murmured.

Her eyes lowered to the floor, toying with the pleats in her dress pants, so she didn't have to look at me.

"Why would you think they'd do that, Karen? Is there something that they don't know?"

She glanced up at me with bloodshot eyes like she was about to cry, but she blinked her tears away before they could fall. Her frizzy hair was also a tell-tale sign that she was, as I suspected, very hungover. She nodded, taking a deep breath, and I braced myself for what she was about to tell me.

"A few days leading up to her disappearance, Jade and I had this big fight," she said, sniffling.

"About what?"

"I knew that my event-planning skills would be useful to her especially after all the dinners I threw when Tony and I were still together. We were talking about me joining her business since she's a hotshot influencer and I thought it'd be a great opportunity since she was getting so much attention from investors. She didn't want me to join, and I was angry. I did something I shouldn't have."

"What did you do?" I asked, curiously.

"I threatened to tell David about it. Look, I know that was wrong. Jade made it clear to all of us girls that she and David were nearly done, I mean she was already lawyered up right? And that he would sabotage her new business the same as he did her last one, right? I know things have been bad for the both of them for a while, but I was just being a bitch. Now, I'm worried that the cops are going to think that I had something to do with her disappearance," she confided in me.

"Karen. With everything going on, I think it's best you tell the cops before they have a reason to suspect you. You keeping it a secret is only going to make them more suspicious."

"I-I don't think I can do that."

Karen's eyes darted around the room quickly like she was nervous I'd find something. I let it go, trying to convince myself that I was just being paranoid, but there was something about the encounter that just didn't sit right with me. I heard a *ding!* on my cell phone once I made it back into the hallway and I checked my email to see that there was a package for Aaron. *It must be those shirts I ordered for him when he landed that new deal a few weeks ago.*

When Aaron first told me that things were finally picking

up at work, where he was making deals that would set us up for a lifetime, I was excited. It wasn't until I realized just how often he'd be gone that it started to worry me. When we moved into Playa Vista Towers, we'd been so excited to start a life together, but now those plans seemed to be at an indefinite halt. *Maybe if I could give him a child, things wouldn't be this way. Maybe we would be more connected as a family,* I thought, riding the elevator down to the lobby.

The receptionist in the lobby handed the package to me. I signed my name on the little electronic pad before heading back to the elevators. I heard a familiar voice coming from the back room where they kept the apartment keys locked for showings. Out came Didi in her expensive suit and new Jimmy Choos that practically made her tower over me. I smiled, noticing the bunches of keys in her hand, and one was tagged "maintenance."

Is that a master key? I asked myself, smiling at her the moment she realized I was standing there.

"Oh Mia! Great. Can you hold these for me for a quick second? The receptionist has something I need to sign and my clients are going to be here any second."

I set the package down on the little glass table by the flowers near the elevator, taking the bunches of keys from her for a moment.

"Of course, Didi."

"Thank you. Oh my God. Thank you."

She rushed off and the sound of her heels got fainter with every step.

I glanced down at the keys in my hand, clutching the little label, and my mind wandered off to the thought of Karen's apartment. *She has to be hiding something. I don't think she's going to ever come right out and tell me. Should I just look for myself? No. That would be wrong. If it helps find Jade, then it has to be worth a shot, right?*

I stood there debating for the next few moments, deciding

to slide the maintenance key into my pocket just as I heard the sound of heels approaching. Didi had her client with her, smiling graciously before leading them to the elevator.

"Thank you," she whispered again.

"Anytime."

I watched as they piled into the elevator, the doors closed, and I took a deep breath. *Maybe this will give me the chance I need to take a look at that apartment Jade had. There had to be something in there that would give me a clue as to what happened the night she disappeared. There has to be.*

～

I had been opening up the packages on the coffee table when I got a call on the landline. I put down the dress shirts in my hands, rushing over to answer it before it stopped ringing.

"Hello?"

"Good evening, Mia. I just wanted to remind you about your massage appointment this evening. I look forward to seeing you again," said the receptionist down at *The Oasis*.

"Oh my God, it completely slipped my mind."

I thought about it for a moment, realizing Aaron wasn't going to be back for the next few hours, and I knew I could use the time to relax.

"I can reschedule it for you if you'd like."

"Thank you, Vic, but I'll make the appointment."

"Wonderful. See you then."

I grabbed my things, and took the elevator down to The Oasis Spa. From the moment I opened the door, I was immediately hit by the scent of lavender in the air. Calming music played overhead and I heard a faint familiar voice near the check-in desk. There was Karen, getting ready for her hour-long massage after we'd just talked about Jade. She didn't so much as turn around to look my way as Victoria led her to the back where her massage bed had to be waiting.

I felt a strange chill roll through the back of my spine, and I wondered what else Karen could've possibly been hiding in that quaint, comfortable apartment of hers. *I guess I'll soon find out.* I thought about the maintenance key that was safely tucked away in the foyer credenza drawer, knowing that breaking into a friend's apartment was going to be the wildest thing I'd ever done in my entire life. *I promised myself that I'd do whatever it takes to find out the truth about Jade. Now I finally understand what that means.*

Victoria came back out in her comfortable slacks, her hair pulled back into a brown claw clip. Her plated name tag caught a glint of light whenever she moved.

"Mia, right this way."

She led me down the dark, calming hallway to my room. I set my things down getting ready for my massage, and I could already tell that I'd be spending the rest of my evening in the sauna. The massage was exactly what I needed and when it was over, I felt relaxed for the first time in ages.

"You were awfully tense today, Mia. Is everything alright?" asked my massage therapist.

"Just a bit stressed it seems. Thank you for this," I murmured.

He smiled at me, grabbing the towels from the corner of the room, and made his way out the door, shutting it behind him. I slipped into the clean, fluffy robe, and changed into a towel the moment I got near the sauna. I was looking forward to being enveloped by the steam.

I opened the door to find a familiar face in the corner and she looked up at me with a smile.

"Mia!"

"Brenda. Hello," I said, softly.

"Girl, hey. Running into just about everyone tonight. How have you been doing?"

We both kept our voices low despite being the only ones in the sauna. I was glad it was only the two of us. It was a chance to talk about this crazy presidential election, about the daily frustrations we felt being one of just a few people of color in this little village we called home. Prior to this year, we thought we were in a progressive, liberal town. Everyone got along beautifully. But now the micro-aggressions were intensifying, and we both realized that something had truly shifted, and not in a good way. Thank God for The Oasis. It was a break away from the world outside, the crazy shit we'd all been through in 2020. Almost everything about our lives was different now, but I was glad that we could still hold onto the little indulgences that made every day a little easier. *It still feels nice being stuck in our little bubble of luxury and conveniences. We all feel safe here, or at least we did until we lost Jade,* I thought, trying to shake it off, because I didn't want to ruin how good I truly felt for once.

"I'm doing great, Brenda. Who else was here?"

"Oh, it was just Karen. She was talking my ear off about planning parties for the next two months. She is so excited that she was able to get an in over at The Honest Company. All of those millenials that work there will be giving her business a big boost- wedding and baby showers for days! Still I'm surprised she can even think about that right now. That's my thing and even I've been struggling ever since - "

"Ever since Jade."

"Yeah. And this damn pandemic, girl. I am over it."'

That's strange. Karen made it seem like she was so distraught by what happened to Jade that the last thing she'd be doing right now is planning next month's events.

"Karen does seem to be one of the few that manages to go on like normal," I murmured.

I watched Brenda's eyebrows raise for a moment before they settled on her face again, and she nodded.

"Yeah, I guess you're right. A lot of us really haven't been the same since."

"Tell me about it. I can't remember the last time I got a good night's sleep. I keep thinking that there's something I'm missing."

"I know what you mean. I wasn't ever really that close with Jade. I mean, we have nothing in common - but she's so sweet. And I know you two are like sisters. From what I hear, the cops aren't really making any progress. I have to say I'm surprised that something like this could happen here, and still no arrests."

"No, they aren't even trying. It's been over a month now and there's still nothing. It's driving me crazy."

"I don't know how someone could up and disappear, especially from a place like this. We literally have cameras in every freakin' place you go."

"Someone knows something. Whoever they are, they're keeping one hell of a secret," I said, and she nodded.

It wasn't exactly the calming evening I was hoping for, because the entire time I was in there, all I could think about was whether Karen was involved in all of this. The more I thought about it, the more I began to make connections I didn't quite see before.

I could understand why Jade didn't want to involve Karen in her business. Karen is flighty and a lightweight lush. Jade's work meant so much to her, and she didn't want there to be any chance of ruining that. *I'm sure Karen didn't take that too well,* I thought. I had to find out the truth, before the curiosity could eat away at me completely, before I start to lose all hope again.

~

"Where have you been? I called you to ask if I should bring dinner," I heard Aaron say as I stepped foot into the apartment.

My eyes widened when I caught sight of him curled up on the couch in sweatpants and a white t-shirt. I could smell the incredible takeout burgers and crinkle fries in the brown paper bag on the kitchen island. I smiled brightly because I couldn't quite remember the last time we did something like this.

"I had no idea you'd be home early tonight. You've been gone every night this week," I reminded him.

I plopped down on the couch next to him and he wrapped his arms around me, kissing the top of my head before I looked up so he could kiss my lips.

"I know, Mia. I'm sorry. Things have been so crazy lately, but I want you to know that I love you. I haven't exactly been the best husband lately, but I'm hoping I can make that up to you. Starting with some seriously greasy food," he said, and I chuckled.

"Oh, Aaron, you really do know the way to my heart, don't you?" I teased.

He made his way to the kitchen to take out two plates, setting out each of the burgers and fries. My stomach rumbled at the scent and it dawned on me that I hadn't eaten much today. I was so wrapped up in the moment that I nearly forgot about the stolen maintenance key hidden in the credenza. *Once I'm done I have to get that key back to Didi. She probably already knows that it's missing. It's okay. It'll be fine. I just need to slip in, find what I'm looking for, and get out.*

Aaron brought the food over to me, curling up on the couch to eat like we used to every Friday evening when we first got married. Now, it was all superbly fancy client dinners and exquisite Michelin-starred cuisine that never quite filled me, or satisfied. As lovely as those fancy dinners are, they made me miss the simple things.

"Thank you for this, Aaron. I needed it."

"Of course, Mia. I love you."

"I love you, too."

8
_____

KAREN

46 Days Missing

𝒥 sat at my vanity in my silk robe, my blonde hair freshly blown out, laying just over my shoulders in soft curls, while I did my makeup. I brushed a light wash of taupe over my eyes and added a soft shade of pink to my lips before I decided on an outfit for the day. My eyes darted to the back of my closet where I'd stashed all of my perfect plans for my next business venture. I didn't even want to look at them anymore ever since Jade shut me down. I was still fuming inside, because I knew the only reason she'd done that was because she was afraid I'd outshine her.

You're not here, Jade. Someone's got to keep everyone happy. I'm sure I can take a whack at the influencing thing and do a much better job than you ever did, I scoffed, rolling my eyes, wondering what the hell even happened to her. The little visit Mia and I had was supposed to make me feel better, but it only made me worry more that the cops were going to drag me away to jail. *I told you because I thought you'd help, Mia. How could you possibly think telling the cops myself is a good idea?*

I shook my head, took a deep breath and gazed at my reflection in the mirror. I noticed that my shoulders still looked a little too tense. *This is what happens when Ivan isn't in to give me my deep tissue massage.*

I pulled out my cell phone and dialed Laura's number, hoping she didn't already have a full day.

"Karen, good morning."

"Good morning, Laura. Any plans today?"

"I-I, no, not really."

"What do you say we head down to *The Oasis* for a massage? I had one yesterday, but I'm still so tense. Please, I could really use the company."

"Uh, okay sure. That sounds lovely."

"Great! I'll get us two spots and I'll text you. See you then!"

I called down to *The Oasis* to hold two spots for us and I made sure I had the right person for the job this time. The spa was only opened to residents at Playa Vista Towers and I was glad for that. The last thing I needed were strangers lurking around. I grabbed my purse, heading out the door.

The spa was even quieter than it was yesterday. Victoria served me a piping hot cappuccino while I waited for my appointment. A few moments later, Laura came strolling in.

"Laura! Please, come sit."

"I'll bring you something to drink as well. What would you like?"

"Tea would be fine, thank you. Anything herbal," she said.

"Not a problem. I'll be right back."

Laura sat down next to me, her purse in her lap, and she looked exhausted.

"Looks like I'm not the only one in need of a massage, after all."

"I guess you can say you called at the right time," she said.

"What's been going on? You're usually the one that's always well-rested and ready to tackle the day."

"Jade. I've been losing so much sleep over the past month and I know I'm not the only one. Mia's having a really hard time, too. I can't imagine what Jade must be going through," she murmured.

"If she's even still alive."

Laura's eyes widened at me and I shrugged. Everyone's been dancing around the elephant in the room since the beginning.

"Why would you say that?"

"Come on, Laura. You can't possibly tell me that thought hadn't crossed your mind. She's been missing for over a month at this point. I miss her as much as the next person, but someone went to an awful lot of trouble to make sure she stayed gone. I mean, wouldn't the cops have found something by now?" I asked.

She stared blankly at me like she couldn't quite process what I was saying, but I knew it was true. *Either the cops are doing a shit job on purpose or there really isn't anything to find. That's only going to make things worse for me. What if they find out about the business proposal? I'll be screwed.*

"I want to believe the cops are doing what they can. Especially with David roaming around aimlessly, it's hard to say where we can really go from here. Soon they're going to start looking at all of us for some kind of information," said Laura.

"You think? They can't do that, can they?"

Laura furrowed her eyebrow at me, studying my expression closely. I glanced around nervously, blowing a little air out of my nose to match the little anxious chuckle.

"Why do you sound so stressed, Karen?"

"I can trust you, right Laura?"

Laura nodded immediately.

"You know you can."

I took a deep breath, telling her about Jade and the business proposal. She listened closely to every detail and I tried to read her eyes to see if she was secretly judging me.

"That was an awful thing you did threatening her like that."

"I know. I would take it all back if I could."

"I think that you need to tell the cops, Karen. It's only going to be worse if they find out on their own."

"Mia said the same thing," I said, sighing.

"Well, she's absolutely right."

"I don't know if I can do it."

"I can go with you this afternoon. No one ever said you have to do this alone," she said, reaching out to place a comforting hand on my knee.

"Thank you, Laura." *Thank God for this massage,* I thought, placing my ceramic cup down on the side table just as Victoria called Laura and me in.

∾

I took a deep breath, walking up the stairs of the police station, feeling the warmth of the Los Angeles sun overhead. This was the first time I'd left the Playa Vista Towers complex in such a long while. It certainly wasn't the kind of outing I was looking forward to.

"I'll be right in the car if you need me."

"Thank you, Laura."

Part of me wanted to turn right around and head back home, but I couldn't. As much as I wanted to keep my mouth shut about the entire Jade thing, if the cops did find out, they'd have no problem tossing me in a jail cell until they found hard evidence. *Ugh. Why did I have to get involved with you, Jade? There's plenty of other business people in the building I could've talked to. I'm sure they would've been much more open to my ideas.*

I tried to shake off how bitter I still was, reminding myself that Jade could've very well been suffering at that very moment. As much of a bitch as she was about the whole business proposal, I wouldn't wish something like that on my worst enemy. I headed to the receptionist's desk, and she looked up at me, so disinterested, like she didn't even care to be there herself.

"Can I help you?"

"Yes, I need to speak to someone about Jade Richardson."

"Who?"

"God. How do you not know? The girl that disappeared at Playa Vista Towers. I have some information that might be useful," I said.

"Wait here."

She rushed back to talk to someone and a few moments later, a man in a clean button-up shirt with the sleeves rolled up and jeans came out to meet me. He was a bit older, but still handsome with his salt and pepper hair. His beard was neat and the scent of cologne let me know that the man had taste. He smelled just like Tony's favorite, Tom Ford. *Maybe I didn't waste a trip down here after all.*

"Hello, my name is Karen. I live at Playa Vista Towers and I'd like to speak to you about my friend, Jade."

"Detective Blanton. It's nice to meet you, Karen. Right this way."

He led me down a long hallway with endless doors and the fluorescent lighting above made the place feel cold. He opened the door to the interrogation room with nothing but a table and two chairs in the very middle of it.

I sat down, the cold metal of the chair freezing the bare skin of my legs. I pressed the wrinkles out of my skirt, looking up at Detective Blanton.

"So, you have information about Jade Richardson."

"Yes, well I didn't think this had anything to do with the investigation, but I decided it was best you hear it from me."

"Oh? Hear what exactly?"

I took him through every last detail and every time he opened up his file to write something down, my heart sank into my stomach. It was like I was waiting for him to look up at me, tell me I basically just confessed to being involved in Jade's disappearance, and haul me off to the nearest jail cell. *Stop it. You're being crazy.*

"Thank you for sharing that with me, Karen. While I'm sure the fight you two had must be hard to deal with now that your friend is gone, it doesn't exactly point me in the direction of a lead."

"Wait, so you're not going to arrest me?"

He chuckled.

"Unless you've done something worth arresting you for, no, I won't."

"Okay, great."

"Though, since David didn't mention Jade's business and you're now telling me that he didn't know about it, it's possible that someone else had."

"Yes! Jade was getting a few calls from some investors that were interested. Honestly, that's what made me want to work with her in the first place. Big opportunity and all that. She ended up picking someone, but she never did tell me who it was. Ugh. If I did know, I'd definitely tell you," I said.

"Well, if you do find out anything else, feel free to give me a call," he said, handing me his card.

His smirk was captivating and it made me forget why I was even there in the first place, even if it was just for a moment.

"Could I use this number to ask you out to dinner some-time?" I waved the card in his direction, then fanned myself with it.

"Let's just stick to sharing information about your friend. My only goal is to find her, okay?"

The seriousness in his voice made me grit my teeth, but I nodded anyway, making my way out of the interrogation room.

"Have a nice day, Karen."

"You too, Detective Blanton," I murmured, practically rolling my eyes as I walked out the front door.

I got back into the car where Laura was blasting the air conditioning and listening to the radio. I could see why because it was absolutely scorching outside. The moment I slammed the car door shut she stared at me expectantly.

"Well? How did it go?"

"He didn't seem like he's going to be putting me in hand-cuffs anytime soon. That Detective Blanton is hot. I tried to flirt with him, but he didn't bite. I guess cops really aren't my type anyway," I said.

"I think you should stick to people that aren't involved in the investigation of our friend, huh?"

"Yeah, I guess you're right. Thanks for coming with me, Laura. I was really scared walking in there."

"Of course, Karen. I'm glad to be here for you," she said.

I smiled softly while she drove us back home. We parted ways at the automatic doors because I had a few packages waiting to be picked up at the receptionist's desk. I signed for them, stacking them one on top of the other, before rushing off to the elevator. Right before I could make it around the corner, someone bumped into me, and they all fell right out of my hands.

"Oh, I'm sorry," I heard him say.

I looked down to see Tony going to grab my package and I nearly snatched it right out of his hand.

"You should be. Those are from Restoration Hardware and they're glass. You better not have broken them," I snapped.

"I'm sorry, Karen."

I hated to admit that he looked as good as he always did. His muscles bulged out of his tank top and he was still sweating probably after a long gym session. I remembered what it was like having those strong muscles wrapped around me, but now that was a thing of the past. *Now he's dating that perfect little conservative bitch*, I thought.

"It's fine. How's the food truck been?"

"It's been good. Things are finally starting to pick up again since things are reopening. It's about damn time," he said, his New York accent thick and hard to ignore.

It made me realize I missed hearing him shout from the food truck window, barking out orders to the staff behind him, and watching as he got his hands dirty cooking up some of the most decadent Italian food I'd ever had. Now that he was with Kate, it made me hate being alone even more, but that wasn't going to stop me from pulling on a few heartstrings where I could.

"I miss those meatballs," I said, and my stomach rumbled.

"We're pulling up out front tonight. I can get you some on the house to make up for whatever the hell I just broke," he said.

"I'd love that."

"See ya."

I smiled, knowing that even though it felt painfully awkward to be talking to him at all, I appreciated the gesture. Tony and I had a lot of history and I was definitely in the mood to remind him of that later tonight. *Let's just hope I don't run into his girlfriend,* I thought, rolling my eyes as I rode the elevator up to my floor.

～

I slipped into a short black dress with satin ties at my shoulder and a scoop neck that made my breasts look incredible. I pulled my icy blonde hair back into a low bun, slipped on my heels then grabbed my leather jacket and purse. *It's time to remind Tony what he's really missing out on right now.*

I could smell the scent of incredible Italian food wafting through the lobby when I made it outside to see the stunning set-up Tony had. He had set out a few picnic tables six-feet apart from each other, the fountain was running in the background, the fairy lights overhead made the place feel warm and inviting. I heard him calling out orders from the window, like he always did, and I knew he was sweaty, hot, and real handsome back there.

I lined up, my eyes glinting in the warm lighting overhead, as he looked over at me.

"Meatballs. As promised."

"Thank you, Tony," I said, softly.

"If you want seconds you're gonna have to pay for it. We are runnin' a business here," he teased, and I laughed.

"You bet."

I found a seat, enjoying my meatballs, and I could overhear the table near me talking.

"Isn't this the building that girl disappeared from?"

"Yeah! It's wild."

"How did you even find out about this place?" one of them asked.

"I saw the food truck posted on Twitter. Food's damn good. Not sure what happened to that girl though. Twitter says it's gotta be her husband."

"Nah, I think it's gotta be someone else. He looked so sad in all those pics online."

I got a light tap on the shoulder moments later and I turned around to see Tony standing there with more meatballs in his hand.

"I thought you said I had to pay for these," I said.

"Yeah, well, we had extra. I'm glad that we can do this, Karen."

"Do what?" I asked, my eyes twinkling at the thought of what he could mean.

"Be friends. It's nice to talk to you when you're not acting like a raging bitch."

I rolled my eyes at him, enjoying our slightly awkward yet comfortable little talk. The other table only grew louder by the minute, chatting about Jade like it was a tabloid story about some wild celebrity.

"That shit's crazy, huh?"

"Tell me about it. I can't believe she's gone."

"I can't believe no one knows where the hell she went or

what happened to her by now. God, if something like that happened to Kate, I don't know what I'd do," he said, and I scoffed.

"What?"

"Nothing, nothing. You two are good together, I guess. I always imagined that you'd find yourself a woman with a bit of edge. Not someone who spends her day wearing ridiculous skirt suits and prances around trying to be a politician," I snapped.

I heard someone clear their throat behind me and when she removed her mask, I realized it was Kate. I didn't even bother trying to take back what I said because I meant every single word.

"Hello, Kate."

"Karen. What are you doing here?"

"Oh, I'm just chatting with Tony after he gave me some free meatballs. You know when we used to - "

"No, I don't want to know. Tony, don't you need to be back there in the food truck?"

"Yeah. Yeah, I should go," he said.

I waved at him smiling, but he only pressed his lips together furiously. I chuckled lightly just as Kate took the seat in front of me.

"You do know you can't just sit anywhere anymore, right? There are rules. You're a little too close for my comfort," I spat.

"I'm going to need you to stay the hell away from me and Tony, Karen. I don't know what sick and twisted game you're playing here, but it needs to stop. Don't ruin my life just because you hate your own."

She stormed off, leaving me alone at the table, and at that moment I realized she may have just been right. I stared at the table who'd been chatting about Jade and they glanced back at me, whispering about what they'd just seen. *Great. Am I the next big piece of gossip?*

9

MIA

47 Days Missing

𝓘 tossed and turned beneath the silk sheets, my loose black curls spread out on the pillow, and a few of them brushed up against Aaron's face. He slept so calmly next to me no matter what time he came strolling in through the front door. I envied that. Every time I closed my eyes, I thought about Jade. I thought about all the secrets she may have been hiding, little pieces to the puzzle that would help me uncover what happened to her. It was like I barely knew her at all.

The sun started pouring into our bedroom when I finally gave up on trying to sleep. I slipped out of bed and Aaron didn't move an inch. I ran a hot shower, letting the water wash away yet another sleepless night. When I finally stepped out, I could smell the scent of fresh coffee wafting from the kitchen.

"You're still home, I'm happily surprised." I said, sauntering over for a kiss.

"I have a meeting in an hour. Another meeting that requires a new suit and with a man that can't stop day drinking."

"Well, I'm sure you'll be able to charm him into whatever you're trying to get him to sign," I teased.

"Here's hoping."

Aaron poured me a cup of piping hot coffee and I downed it all in one go, burning the roof of my mouth ever so slightly.

"Whoa there. What are you fueling up for?"

"Nothing. Nothing. I just need something to wake me up is all," I murmured nervously.

He didn't seem to notice that I was practically fumbling around the kitchen to make sure he didn't venture off into the foyer to the credenza for anything. *The last thing I need is Aaron asking me any questions I can't answer.* He was pretty wrapped up replying to emails on his phone before planting a kiss on my lips and heading off to the bathroom. I was just about to go snag the key from the credenza when he turned around to face me.

"Hey, Mia - "

"Y-Yes?"

"Is everything okay?" he asked, wrinkling his eyebrows. Standing in our kitchen in the bright light of day, I realized how very lucky I am. Aaron has been distant at times, but he works so hard to provide this amazing life for us, and he is a gorgeous man.

"Yes, of course everything is okay. Why wouldn't it be?"

"Maybe you should lay off the coffee, after all."

"Right."

"Oh, before I forget, Tony's bringing the food truck around just for the crew tonight. We won't have to deal with any strangers and I know how much you love his gnocchi. I'll be back around nine, but if I'm late, just go without me and I'll meet you there. Sound good?"

"Yeah. See you then."

My stomach rumbled, but I knew I wouldn't be able to eat anything until I did what I needed to do. *What the hell is going to happen to me if Karen catches me breaking into her place? She's never going to let it go, and I'm probably going to end up in jail! No. Calm down. It's going to be fine.*

I waited until I heard the shower turn on and I grabbed the key from the credenza, slipping it into my purse on the chaise lounge for later. *The only reason I'm doing this is because I need to find out what happened to you, Jade. There's something Karen's not telling me.*

I checked the time on my phone screen and it was nearing seven o'clock. I had just enough time to change and slip out the front door before Karen would take off for her morning spin class. The funny thing about being neighbors in a building like Playa Vista Towers is that you know each other's every move. I made it into the elevator, heading down to her floor, hoping I didn't run into anyone I knew on the way.

Karen's hallway was quiet when I arrived at her front door. There wasn't anyone around and I pressed my ear up against the wooden exterior to see if I could hear her walking around in there. It was absolutely silent and I took a deep breath, turning the maintenance key in the lock, grabbing the door handle and turning it slowly. Her apartment was completely empty and I set my purse down, getting ready to search every corner until I found something.

I started in the living room, looking through the decorative shelves, the stack of old DVDs she was still holding onto, and the three fashion print coffee table books near the remote on the television console. Karen lived in her glory days, when she was head cheerleader in college, when she was a Lakers girl, but most of all, when she believed that Tony was going to marry her and get his famous producer friends to cast her in a blockbuster movie.. That didn't work out, but she kept her head up, moving on to the next scheme. You had to admire her sheer determination, even if you hated her actual desperation. She was ambitious and jaded at the same time, and therefore exhausting to be around. I made my way into her bedroom, going through her closet, but there was nothing in there but a bunch of clothes with the tags still attached. I nearly tripped over the new shopping bags she had yet to unpack, but when I finally sauntered over to her desk, my heartbeat quickened.

I saw a large black binder sitting underneath the latest issue of Vogue, and when I opened it up, it contained Karen's business proposal. It had just about every plan she had worked on, including the one she was sure Jade would jump on as the opportunity to make her business a collaborative effort. Karen, Karen, Karen. Why did she think Jade would want to ever partner with her, of all people, to share the spotlight? Did she not understand how extremely competitive this YouTube business model was?

Or maybe she did. As I flipped through, there were pages torn out, scribbles just about everywhere, and I noticed that she scratched Jade's name out at the very front. In blood red ink. Next to it she wrote something that made my stomach turn. *"Someone's going to replace you, bitch."* I wanted to believe it was written in anger. I wanted to believe that Karen was just lost in a whirlwind of jealousy, but I started to wonder if she really had something to do with Jade's disappearance.

Who did you expect would replace her, Karen? You? I took photos on my phone of every page I could, doing a quick sweep of the rest of Karen's hot mess of an apartment before glancing down at the time, realizing I had to go, now! I could've sworn I heard footsteps in the hallway. Shit. *Shit. Shit. Shit.* I put everything back where it was, rushed out, and locked the door behind me.

~

I hurried down the corridor to the elevator and when my fingertips finally found the button, I could've sworn I heard footsteps coming from behind me. I glanced around, but there was no one there. I had an extremely eerie feeling in my head and a strong sense in my gut, that I was being watched, that someone knew what I had just done, but I told myself that I was just being paranoid. Once the elevator doors shut, I clicked the button to the tenth floor, hoping I could get in to see what Jade was hiding in that apartment of hers. I had to summon all of my courage to keep going.

It felt strange that she didn't even mention this apartment, because as far as I knew, I was the one she told everything to. *I knew about David. I knew about her business. So, why hide this?* I asked myself. There were people waiting to enter the elevator when I got off and they seemed to be deep in discussion about something only to clam up the minute they saw me. I shook it off, walking down the carpeted hallway to the right unit. I stuck the maintenance key inside, but the door wouldn't give. I tried a few more times, even going as far as to slam my entire body up against it, but it was jammed.

That can't be possible. This key is supposed to open every single door for at least the first ten floors. I thought, remembering that the key had a little *"1-10"* written on it. It frustrated me that I couldn't get in, that there could be secrets hidden behind that door that could lead me to the truth. I sighed, heading down to the lobby, turning the corner to the back room so I could drop the maintenance key on the floor behind the concierge desk. The concierge definitely has already left at this hour, and is probably drinking with the rest of the staff over at The Vine. *Oh no, what if the cameras catch it, but if I am discreet and nonchalant, and pay attention to the camera location, it's possible to pull this off. My days in acting class do pay off from time to time. Didi will just think she dropped it. Didi knows everything about these apartments, so if Jade owned that one, she'd have to know about it, right?*

I started devising a new plan on the way back home, because I knew I couldn't just come right out and tell Didi I've been snooping. *I'll figure it out. I have to. I just know there's something worth finding in that place. Why else would Jade have kept it a secret?*

∼

The fairylights twinkled overhead as Tony got the food truck up and running for our little social club's dinner outdoors. I could smell the intoxicating scent of fresh pasta and basil in the air, and it felt good that it was just the few of us, the closest of our neighbors, gathering around to enjoy. I had a feeling that David would show up eventually, and it was going to take every ounce of self-control left in me not to jump right down his throat again, but I promised myself I'd try. I was enjoying my wine in a little paper cup when I heard footsteps approach from behind me.

"Mia. I was hoping I'd see you tonight."

"Laura, how are you? It's been a while. You look great! I love the new hair color!" I said. enthusiastically. Laura was fond of adding a streak of blue to the tips of her hair, or going all pink. Even though she could technically take advantage of shopping during Senior Hours, Laura did not give an inch to aging. She fought it every step of the way, and successfully. Laura's clothes were trendy as hell, she was up on all of the latest and greatest reality tv shows, and she loved a good party.

"I'm as great as I can be. Have you heard anything else about Jade?"

I shook my head, wishing I had some good news to share, but all I had were more questions. Karen's black binder burned a hole in my mind, but I tried not to think too hard about it.

"Nothing yet. It's been so long and the cops seem to have no leads. I don't know what else to do."

"All we can do now is hold out hope."

I smiled warmly at her, knowing that wasn't enough for me. I spotted Karen exiting the automatic doors, stepping out in her strappy heels and little black dress, heading straight for Tony. I watched the way she flirted with him, the way she didn't even care that Kate was standing right there. She looked like she was having a grand time, and it made me think that everything she told me had been a lie. *Do you really even care that Jade's missing? Does anyone?*

I was eating my way through some fluffy focaccia bread and sipping on my wine when I felt two warm hands press against my bare shoulders.

"Aaron! You're here!"

I turned around to kiss him hard and I could feel him smile through it.

"Of course. I tried to wrap things up as fast as possible so I could be here with you. Have you had your gnocchi yet?"

"Not yet."

"Let me go grab some for you."

I watched as my husband rolled up his sleeves, smiling and greeting every single one of our friends. He was charming, and it came so naturally. I knew that one day he planned to be a candidate for office- local or even national- but he was the type of man to lay out a foundation, gather together his troops and then make a sneak attack when the time was right. I don't think anyone else knew his ultimate ambition, but I knew he wanted to be at the top, by any means. I tried not to judge his ambition, and he tried not to judge my lack of. We were happy this way, weren't we?

It was nice to see them all together again, going about their lives the way they always had, but I couldn't. I wondered if there would ever be a time where I could finally move on, and part of me worried that I'd never get the answers I was so desperately looking for. *You can't think that way. The truth is out there. Someone out there knows something, and it could very well be anyone here.*

Aaron brought me a takeout box and a fork. I opened it up and took in the scent of fresh lobster gnocchi, sharing it with him. We were all about to wrap up for the night when I caught Aaron staring at David who'd finally decided to make an appearance. He reeked of alcohol, stumbling around, and his foot got caught on one of the picnic tables. He fell face first on the pavement, busting his lip open.

Aaron rushed to help him, but he swatted his arms away.

"I don't need your fucking help, okay? Get away from me, bro. I'm fine. Stay the hell away from me. I came because I heard Tony was passin' out free food. That right, Tony?"

"Not to your drunk ass. Look, I know you're going through a tough time, bud, but you can't be doing this," said Tony. Tony's cheekbones were hardening and flexing. All of that gym time had him ready to fight, and he would happily take David down to the gutter, where almost everyone felt he belonged anyway, if not a lower place.

"You don't know a damn thing about what I'm going through. None of you do!"

David helped himself to his feet, scrambling back inside while we all stared at the automatic doors. The blood that had dripped from his lips lay in a small puddle where he'd fallen and I knew that was certainly going to stain.

"Come on, Mia. Let's go," said Aaron, wrapping his arm around me.

He led me back to the lobby and in his arms, I felt truly safe.

I sat at my vanity in my silk robe, pulling my hair back with a headband so I could slather a face mask on and hopefully relax. Aaron was in the living room answering emails and it felt good to have him around. I carefully smoothed the light pink cream on my face, letting it sit while I basked in the warm light of our bedroom. I tried to put David's outburst out of my mind, but it only made me wonder whether he really did have something to do with this or if he was as in the dark as the rest of us.

He's done some crazy things but I've never seen him act that way, I thought, crawling into bed with a novel to read. I only got a few pages in before I realized that my mind was running a little too wild to relax. I grabbed my laptop from my desk, opened up a fresh document, and let the words flow from my fingertips. The document was filled with a mess of my thoughts, all of the pieces I'd learned so far, and every secret I'd uncovered that only made me wonder how much I really knew my best friend.

This is going to drive me insane. I should at least try to get some sleep tonight. I washed my face mask off and tossed my silk robe on the chair in the far corner of the room. I slipped beneath the sheets, dozing off almost instantly.

I woke up. The world around me was still dark. I glanced over at the alarm clock on the nightstand to see that it was just after four o'clock. I got up and went out to the kitchen for a glass of water. The cool liquid felt incredible trickling down my throat. When I returned to bed, my phone screen lit up with a soft buzz. *Who in the world could be texting me at this hour?* I asked myself. I nearly tried to go back to sleep without checking it, but before I could doze off again, I grabbed my phone from the nightstand.

I opened up the text message and it read:

Mia. It's me, Jade. I'm okay. I know you're trying to help, but you need to stop looking. It'll only make things worse. Please.

My eyes widened immediately and any ounce of sleepiness I had completely disappeared. I didn't recognize the number the text came from, but I called it anyway. I listened to it ring, hoping that Jade would pick up. My heart was beating so loudly in my chest that I really thought I was about to pass out.

"Jade. Jade, pick up, please," I whispered.

I felt Aaron stirring next to me and he placed his hand on my back, rubbing it softly before he sat up in bed with me. I clutched the phone tightly in my hands, feeling the tears well up behind my eyes.

"What's going on?"

"Aaron. Read this," I said, handing him my cell phone.

He furrowed his brow, squinting as the grogginess slowly left his body, and he glanced back at me with wide eyes.

"What the hell? When was this sent?"

"Sometime when we were asleep I guess. Do you think it could be real? Do you think someone's messing with me?"

"I don't know what to think, Mia."

His voice was low and emotionless, like he didn't even care that this could very well be the break in the case the cops needed. I reread the text a few times, trying to figure out if I should tell the cops, or if that was only going to make things more difficult. *They're not doing much to find her. They should be here. We should be out searching the entire complex. Search parties, flyers, billboards, something.*

The text message made my stomach turn. I couldn't decide if it was really Jade or not and if I was going to keep this a secret, I needed to know why. My fingertips quickly moved across my phone screen as I texted her back.

If you want me to stop looking, Jade, I need to know why. I need to know what's going on. How do I know this is even you?

I hit send and put the phone back on my nightstand so I wouldn't stare at it endlessly waiting for a response. Aaron sat there with me, pressing his lips against my hair softly, but it didn't comfort me this time.

"Do you think I should tell the police?"

"I think you should do whatever you feel is right, Mia. If this really is Jade, talking to the cops might screw things up for her, but if it's not - "

"Then I could be wasting time when I should be looking for my best friend."

"I know you'll make the right decision, whatever you choose," said Aaron.

94

I nodded, taking a deep breath, leaning over to kiss him before my head hit the pillow again. My eyes stayed open until sunrise, but at some point, while I'd been lost in thought about Jade, I fell asleep.

I woke up at eight o'clock, my eyelids fluttering open slowly before what happened finally came rushing back. I grabbed my phone frantically, hoping that I got a response, but when I looked through my messages, there was nothing there. I glanced over at Aaron who was still fast asleep, and I sat there in bed completely bewildered. *There's no way I imagined the whole thing. Where the hell could the text have gone? Text messages don't just disappear! Aaron's still asleep. He fell asleep before I did. So, who deleted the text?*

My heartbeat quickened and I began to worry that this was far more complicated than I initially thought. I wondered if Jade really was out there, running from someone or something that terrified her. *Whatever it is, Jade, I won't stop. I won't stop looking until I know the truth. The truth starts with that apartment.*

10

DIDI

48 Days Missing

I pressed the button on my new espresso machine, listening to it whir as my decadent, dark coffee filled my glass mug. I pulled my hair back into a clean bun, feeling the excitement rush through me at the thought of matching my clients with their perfect new space. *Call me a goddamn matchmaker,* I thought. I opened up my laptop at the breakfast bar, queuing up a few social posts to go live. I decided to give the whole social media thing a go after seeing Jade's success. I thought it'd be a great way to drum up some business. *I wish you were here, Jade. I don't even know what a good video looks like.*

One of the last conversations Jade and I had was about filming some clips for my website. She was so thrilled to be helping and so damn good at what she did. *No wonder you were getting so much attention, Jade. You were a real natural. The camera loves you. I just hope it gets the chance to love you all over again.*

I sighed, downing my espresso so fast it felt like it burned a damn hole in my tongue. I slipped my laptop and files into my crocodile-patterned work tote. *Vegan leather really is a game changer.* I checked the time on my Tiffany watch to see I was still a half hour too early before I had to meet my clients in the lobby. That's when I heard a knock on my front door. I glanced through the peephole to see Mia standing there with her beautiful natural curls and warm skin. I unlocked the door, opened it up, and she smiled warmly at me.

"Good morning, Didi. Oh, is now a bad time? You look like you were just about to head out."

"I have some time to spare. What brings you by?"

"Well, I was actually hoping you'd help me find a unit. See I've been thinking that Aaron and I need a bit more space because I could use an office, too. He takes up all that we have and I don't really feel like sacrificing the guest bedroom. You get that, right?"

"Oh my God, of course! What were you thinking? You know what? No. I have the perfect unit for you. It's on the forty-ninth floor! The views are insane," I said.

I couldn't contain how giddy I was because the moment any one of my friends mentioned it was time to purchase a new place, it practically made my heart flutter.

"You just say the word and I'll take care of everything. I'm sure we can get your place sold in no time. Everyone's dying to live here."

"I was actually thinking of staying a little closer to the ground. Maybe the tenth floor. I heard great things about the view in 1002."

"Where in the world did you hear that from?" I asked, completely baffled.

Mia shifted around, fidgeting with her fingers, and I raised an eyebrow at her. She parted her lips ready to tell me and I couldn't wait to hear how she could've possibly got information about that unit.

"It belongs to Jade. That's how I know about it and I know you do, too. You must know because you're the only person that would've sold her that unit," said Mia.

I shook my head, wrinkling my eyebrows.

"That unit doesn't belong to Jade. Now I'm intrigued. Why would you think it did?"

"The portfolio with all of Jade's work, press, and media clippings. There were some letters and bills in the very back that she must've forgotten to take out. It was addressed to that unit with her name on it."

"That's not possible," I murmured.

Mia lowered the strap of her Saint Laurent tote bag, reaching in for the portfolio. She handed it to me and I flipped through all the mail tucked into the back pocket. *Oh my God. She's right.*

"1002 belongs to one of the investors in the building, but I don't even know which one, myself."

"I need to get in to see it, Didi. There could be something in there that will help us figure out what happened to her. Don't you want that? Don't you want things to go back to the way they were? Life would be so different if Jade was here. We'd be spending our time indoors baking banana bread and doing a whole lot of online shopping. Instead, we have no idea where she is. Please," Mia begged.

"Mia, I want to help, I do, but if I take you into that unit without authorization I could lose my license."

Mia folded her arms at her chest, taking a deep breath, and I already knew what she was going to say.

"You could lose your license, but what's Jade got to lose? Practically everything if we don't figure out what happened to her."

I sighed, nodding.

"Come back here around midnight. We'll go up there together and hope to God that there's no one inside. I'll ask around, see what I can find out. Mia, I need you to keep this between us, okay? If we find anything, we have to go to the cops and tell them that Jade was using the unit, nothing more. I can't upset the investors in this building otherwise I'll never be able to show a unit here or anywhere else ever again."

"Of course, Didi. Thank you."

"Don't thank me yet. Let's just hope there's really something to find."

~

I finally made it home after a long day of showings, kicked off my heels, and poured myself a glass of wine. I heard my laptop *ping!* I rushed over to see if the email I had sent earlier had a response. *Come on. Someone's got to know something about this mysterious unit,* I thought, scrolling to the top, and clicking the most recent notification. I opened it up, reading it over carefully, while I sipped on my glass of red.

The unit was sold just over two years ago, but as far as Philip, my realtor friend, knew, no one was living there. *How did Jade even find out about it? Was the investor that owned the place the one who was interested in Jade's career?*

I sent a quick email back asking Phil for any more information, knowing he'd have a dozen questions for me when I saw him tomorrow morning. I glanced over at the clock on the side of my television screen. I had just over two hours to kill before I had to get right back into my heels and break into an apartment in the building. *I guess there's a first time for everything.*

I was just about to change into something a little more comfortable when I heard a knock on the door. I sighed, rushing over to open it.

"Mia, what are you doing here this early? I thought I told you - "

"Not Mia."

I stared at Kate standing in my doorway with a basket of freshly baked muffins. She furrowed her brow at me, probably wondering what that little outburst was about.

"Have a night out planned with Mia? It's already pretty late, isn't it?"

"Oh, yes. She asked that I watch that new thriller with her

because Aaron's going to be working late. I'm not the biggest thriller movie fan," I said, raising my wine glass to her.

She handed me the basket and I began to relax a little, knowing that even though my life was about to get a whole lot wilder, there was still a little normalcy left.

"I just wanted to bring these because you did such an amazing job finding the perfect new home for Tony and me. Things are really getting serious between us, and I wouldn't be surprised if he popped the question real soon."

"That's amazing! It really is. Thank you so much for this, Kate. You didn't have to go through all that trouble," I said.

"Nonsense. It's the least I can do. I would've brought them by sooner, but Tony and I got into a little argument."

"Oh, no. What happened?"

"He's been watching conspiracy theory videos again. I swear, doesn't he know the government is doing everything they can to protect the people? Working for Eric Giovanni really showed me just how determined everyone is to help life get back to normal."

"Yeah, well I'm not sure I even know what normal is anymore," I confessed.

"Hey, look on the bright side. The real estate market is booming and I hear you've been getting clients nonstop," said Kate.

"I have. It's been great. At least I have something to preoccupy myself so I don't end up watching conspiracy theory videos myself," I teased.

"Oh, no. Not you, too. Speaking of, Tony and I were watching a few of Jade's old vlogs. It's crazy how much life has changed, huh? You should take a look at her comment section. Everyone's so worried about her. Hell, she's got thousands of people wondering where she is and the cops still don't seem to have any answers."

"All we can do is hope she finds her way home. When she does, life will be that much sweeter, won't it?"

"It sure will."

"Take care, Kate."

"You too, Didi."

I shut the door, heading back to the breakfast bar where my laptop was sitting, and I started scrolling through Jade's old videos. I loved seeing how happy she looked and how simple life used to be. She had a smile that could light up any room, a vibrant, bubbly personality that made being around her such a wonderful time. I missed how she'd get her camera out at lunch to document what we had, the amazing fashion shows she'd drag us to, and the nightlife she'd share that took LA by storm.

It was like she lived a double life. I remembered how quiet, shy, and timid she'd be whenever she was with David. It was amazing that she kept her social media life a secret for as long as she did, but I knew that David was probably too drunk to even realize what was going on. I was surprised he was even able to handle work during the day. *Now I understand why Jade and David never went out together. Anniversaries passed, Valentine's Day, birthdays, but they never stepped foot inside a restaurant together after they got married.*

Now that David knew the truth, now that he understood how many people out there were rooting for her to make it home, he had to know that he wouldn't be able to keep what happened a secret forever. *Am I jumping the gun by thinking he's the one that did this? He's a bad guy, yes, but bad enough to hurt Jade? I don't know.*

I shut my laptop screen, glancing over at the master key sitting near my purse, and I took a deep breath. *Mia's right. We need to find something. We need to bring her home.*

~

"Are you sure no one followed us? I swear I heard footsteps down the hall on the other side," said Mia.

"I checked, double-checked, and triple-checked. The hallway cameras were facing the other way, too. We don't want anyone knowing we were here. Got it?"

Mia gulped, nodding. I took the key out of my Burberry trench coat pocket, slipped it in the keyhole and turned it slightly. I felt the little click and my hand wrapped around the door handle. The subtle creak of the hinges scared me, but I opened it up to a stuffy apartment that looked like it hadn't been touched in months. I fumbled for the light switch, and to my surprise, the place was perfectly furnished. It looked like someone took their time decorating the place, not like it had been staged for a showing. My heart practically skipped a beat when I began recognizing the backgrounds of all of Jade's videos. I never really gave much thought to where she'd filmed them, but now I knew.

"So this is where she's been taking the internet by storm, huh?"

"I guess so."

We took a quick glance around before my cell phone started to ring in my pocket. I fished it out, glancing down at the screen to see that it was Philip calling. My heart nearly leaped right out of my chest before it connected.

"Philip? It's late. Is everything okay?"

"I've been doing you a favor, Didi. I owe you one after that last showing fiasco. Look, I couldn't find a name, but I did find out that the investor that owns the unit is coming down there tonight. He should be there any minute. You could try to go get a good look at him. Though, just don't get yourself in trouble, okay?"

"Ah, okay. Thank you so much, Philip! Gotta go!"

I hung up the phone quickly, grabbing Mia by the arm and I hauled her out of there. I locked the door quickly, and she stared back at me confused.

"We need to get out of here. Now!" I yelled at her.

We heard the elevator *ding!* and we bolted straight for the stairwell. We managed to get down to the ninth floor before anyone saw us, and that's when I filled Mia in on what was happening.

"We have to go back up and see who it is! He might know -"

"Stop right there. Look, we'll take what we know to the cops, but I'm not waltzing back up there with my job on the line. Neither are you because someone will figure out I'm involved. We'll go to the cops tomorrow morning. Let them handle it from here."

Mia nodded. We parted ways, and I was somehow still afraid that someone knew what we'd been up to.

I had a showing the next morning for a unit on the tenth floor, and I briefly passed by 1002 afterward to see if there was anything strange happening. I wasn't sure what I was looking for, knowing there wouldn't be much to find by staring at the front door, but I couldn't help myself. Jade was tied to that place, and it made me feel uneasy. I took a good long look at the door when I realized that the door handle wasn't the same aged brass that it was last night. It was brand new, looking like it hadn't been worn in at all, and I looked down to see that the entire lock had been changed. *No. No no no. This can't be happening. God. What did I get myself into?*

I tried to keep my cool making my way down to the lobby in a wrinkly button-up and palazzo pants. I was too flustered to even care how I looked and when I locked eyes with Mia in the lobby, it was like she could tell that I was on the verge of losing my mind.

"What's going on?"

"Mia. Someone changed the locks. I had a showing on the tenth floor this morning and the lock, door handle, everything is brand new."

"That's impossible. We were just there a few hours ago," she reminded me.

"I know. I hope no one saw us. Look, the master key I have isn't going to work anymore. I don't know if there's going to be any getting back into that unit."

"Didi, we have to. There could be something there that - "

"I can't get involved anymore. This is too much, Mia. I could lose everything."

"Then I'll just have to find another way."

I admired just how determined she was, but I knew that if the investors or the owner of that unit even suspected that I was snooping around the place, it'd be over for me. My job, my life, everything I've built would just go up in flames.

"I'll see what I can do to help. Maybe if I get some more information or find out if anyone in the building knows more, it could be a good place to start. I just can't get near the place again."

"I understand, Didi. Thank you. Really," said Mia.

We made our way down to the parking garage and got into my Mercedes, taking off down the winding corners up until we were out on the street. The drive to the police station was quiet, like we were both trying to figure out how something like this could've even happened, and I couldn't shake the feeling that someone knew what we were trying to do. I tried my best to stay calm, and when I pulled up to the station's parking lot, it was like I was frozen.

My hands were shaking, my heart was pounding, and I could feel a single bead of sweat trickle down the back of my neck. I gulped, glancing over at Mia who was clutching Jade's portfolio in her hands.

"I got this. You wait here. There's no reason to get you involved in this. Thank you again, Didi."

I nodded, watching her slide her mask over her face. She hopped out of the car. I turned up the air conditioning to drown out how hot it was, blasting some light R&B while I tried to breathe. My mind was stirring with questions and it all led back to that damn apartment. I couldn't understand why Jade would've kept it a secret, especially from us. *Is this investor someone we know? Why else would she need to hide who it is? If it was just some bigshot LA businessman, surely she would've at least told Mia. What the hell is really going on here?*

11

MIA

49 Days Missing

The interrogation room was hot. I shifted around in my seat trying to get comfortable. The sweat made my hair cling to my forehead and I tapped my fingernails lightly against the portfolio cover, wishing I had a glass of water as the door slowly swung open. In came a man wearing blue jeans and a button-down shirt with the sleeves rolled up. He barely even looked me in the eyes as he sat down, folding his hands with his elbows pressed firmly into the table.

"Mia, is it? I hear you're the one that's always been calling the station," he said.

"Yes, that's me."

"Detective Blanton."

My eyes widened because I realized this was the man that I'd been trying to see for ages, the one that was fresh on the scene ready to solve this case, or so I heard. *All he's done is interview the wrong people. Manny? Come on,* I thought, sliding the portfolio over to him.

"What's this?" he asked.

"That is Jade's portfolio. There's a detailed list of all of the work she's done in the past year alone. In the back there is some mail that's addressed to her, but the apartment number isn't the one she lives at. It isn't her home," I said.

He looked intrigued with his fingers pressed up against his lips, studying the outside of each envelope like they were going to fill in the blanks for him.

"Do you know what she was doing there? Was she seeing someone? Having an affair, perhaps?"

"No. Jade would never do such a thing. Even though David's been a shitty husband, Jade would still never do that. I don't know what this place is, but I'm hoping it'll help you find her," I lied.

Flashbacks of last night hit me like a tidal wave. I was caught in a time warp of standing in that apartment waiting to find something, a clue that would lead me to where Jade could've gone. I didn't get the chance and that was eating away at me more than I'd like it to. *I have to get back in there somehow. Even if Didi can't help me, someone else will. There has to be a way.*

"I'll send some officers down there to take a look. Thank you, Mia."

"No, I think you need to go down there yourself. It's been forty-nine days since Jade went missing and your department has done absolutely nothing to find her. I don't want this getting swept under the rug like everything else. Please, just find my friend," I pleaded.

"We're doing the best we can."

He stayed rather tight-lipped about the whole situation, but I saw his eyes flitting around the room like he knew more than he was letting on. I left the room, exiting the police station as the thick grey clouds collected overhead. It started to pour before I made it back to the car. I realized I couldn't remember the last time it rained like this.

"How did it go?" Didi asked as soon as I opened the car door.

"Detective Blanton said he'd check it out. That's the kind of news that's supposed to comfort me, but it absolutely doesn't. I really don't think they're going to go out of their way to find her," I murmured, grimly.

"So, what are we going to do?"

"We'll figure something out. We have to."

Didi nodded and I could tell that she was worried about what would happen to her career, so much so that she was starting to shut out this little investigation of ours. *No one ever said this was going to be easy, but I'm not giving up. I'm not going to wait for the cops to tell me what happened. I'm going to find out the truth if it's the last thing I do.*

~

I shut my apartment door behind me, peeled off my wet clothes, and my soaked hair clung to my back. I headed to the bathroom to run the shower, washing away everything that had happened in the last twenty-four hours. My mind continued to stir relentlessly and it dawned on me then that there was one way I could check out parts of that apartment. *Jade's videos. So many of them were filmed there. I've seen them all before, but that was before she went missing. That was before I knew there was something to hide.*

I wrapped myself in a fluffy robe and slippers, leaving my wet hair to air dry as the darkness settled in my living room. The thunder cracked loudly, the lightning illuminating my floor-to-ceiling windows as I curled up on the couch with my laptop. My heart started to beat faster when I clicked on Jade's channel name, realizing I hadn't seen her face in such a long time. I knew that it would be hard for me but it was the first real step in finding out where she was. The video started playing, the little red bar making its way across the screen, and I basked in how incredibly happy she looked.

She took her viewers through the new outfits she bought, styling them perfectly. She talked about the home decor tips that were game-changers for her, showing items in a home that definitely wasn't her home with David. *That's the apartment,* I thought, picking up on the artwork on the walls, the playbills, the musical posters. It was like someone had taken New York and plopped it right down in Playa Vista Towers.

Jade always talked about how much she'd love to live in New York for a little while. She wanted to experience the glitz and the glamour of a classic Audrey Hepburn movie. *We promised to take a trip there together once the world returned to normal. It will happen. It has to. I'm going to bring you back home, Jade. Even if I have to do it all by myself.*

I found myself reopening the document I'd been writing in for the past few days, going over all of the details I learned so far. I wrote down everything I remembered about the apartment. From Jade's lavish clothing hauls to the cold emptiness of it when I first stepped foot inside. I wrote about Karen, about the business, the details, every little thing I knew about Jade's life. The pieces didn't seem to fit together, but I knew there had to be a connection somewhere. I felt it in my gut that the person that was responsible for this was someone I knew.

David? Karen? Who else is there? Who did this to you, Jade?

I felt the pressure on my stomach lift and my eyes fluttered open to see Aaron standing over me trying to peer into my laptop screen. I instinctively shut it and he stared at me confused.

"I was trying not to wake you," he said, with a chuckle.

"Uh, how long was I asleep?" I asked, trying to change the subject.

I clutched my laptop to my chest for a moment before sitting it down on the coffee table. Aaron took the seat next to me on the overstuffed Restoration Hardware couch, sliding under the blanket with me. He was still fully dressed with his tie perfectly done up, but I didn't care. He smelled divine and the warmth emanating from his body was enough to calm me down ever so slightly.

"You were asleep when I got home. It's just after midnight now. Are you okay, Mia? You seem a bit startled," he murmured, running his fingers through my hair.

I debated telling him the truth. I thought about what he might say if he learned about the lengths I'd gone to in order to find out what happened to Jade, but I couldn't come right out and say it. He'd been there for me from the very beginning, and I didn't want to involve him in anything that could jeopardize his career or our life. I was the only one without any real strings. I was the one that could push the limits and do what was necessary. *Maybe it's time I put my degree in journalism to good use.*

"I'm alright. Things have just been a little strange around here is all."

"Jade?" he asked.

"Yes. I'm trying to focus on the good, make the most of what I have right now, but it's hard when she may not get the same chance."

"As much as I know you want to find her, Mia, this is destroying you. I think it's time you let Jade go. I think it's time you let all of this go," he said.

"How can you say that? What if it were me, Aaron? What if I was the one that went missing?"

"Don't do that, Mia. You know if something happened to you, I'd spend every waking moment looking for you. I'm just saying, maybe you didn't know Jade as well as you think you did. I mean, if the cops haven't found anything and you got that text from her, maybe she did leave on her own."

"I don't believe that for a second and neither should you."

"Mia, come on."

"No, Aaron. I know Jade. She would've never done something like this. I haven't told the cops about the text message, and now I can't," I said.

"Why not?"

"Because it's gone."

"Gone?"

"I don't know how, but it's not there anymore. Look, we don't have to talk about this, okay? I'm fine. I'm just going to go get some sleep," I snapped.

He didn't try to follow me to bed and I imagined it was because he believed I needed some space. I clutched the pillow hard, trying to figure out where to start looking for answers. *Anyone could know something. Looks like I'll just have to ask every single last one of them until someone cracks.*

A few hours later, the ground started to shake violently, the chandelier overhead started to swing, and I instantly woke up, kicking Aaron awake. We were so high up that we couldn't possibly make it down to the lobby or outside the building at all. Aaron held me tight and we rode it out, until the shaking finally came to a halt. I looked up at Aaron who planted a kiss firmly on my forehead. I took a deep breath, telling myself that I had to have overreacted when we fought. *All he's ever done was be here for me. He just doesn't want to see me implode. I shouldn't involve him in this. I can't just tell him that I'm going to be investigating our friends, can I? Maybe I should. Maybe I should just trust him.*

"Are you okay?"

"I-I think so."

"Mia, I'm sorry. I didn't mean to upset you earlier."

"I'm sorry, Aaron. I know you're just trying to help. You should know that I'm not going to let this go, not until I get some closure. I have a gut feeling that one or our friends has to know something about what happened to Jade. I have to find out the truth, even if it turns out that you're right and I didn't know her as well as I thought I did," I confessed.

"I understand, Mia. I'm here to help. Whatever you need, okay?"

He brought my hand to his lips, kissed them softly, and I smiled. I fell back asleep with ease right there in his arms.

~

I grabbed my Louis Vuitton bag, slinging the strap over my shoulder before making my way to the elevator to head down to the lobby. The fridge was completely empty, and it had been a long time since Aaron and I had a home cooked meal together. I checked my cell phone to see that a text had just come in from him. *I'll be home tonight. On time. I promise.* I smiled, as the elevator doors opened up to the bustling lobby, and I saw Karen standing there with Laura.

"Oh my God, Mia! Did you feel that earthquake last night?"

"Yes, I did. Was there any damage?"

"Well I lost a few thousand dollars in lamps and I'm sure there are other people here who lost more. It's a shame. Tectonic plates and all that," said Karen.

I tried my best not to roll my eyes at her, but Laura seemed to cut the tension immediately.

"Heading out?"

"Just over to the grocery store. Aaron's coming home early tonight so I thought I'd make him something nice," I said.

"Yeah, uh, that sounds nice. Okay, well, I gotta go. Restoration Hardware is open for curbside pickup and I really need some new lamps," Karen chimed in before taking off, the sound of her heels disappearing around the corner as she took the elevator down to the parking garage.

"That was strange."

"Karen always is. I should be taking off, too. I'll see you around, Mia."

"Of course, Laura. Take care."

She smiled cordially at me before heading straight for the side doors out to the courtyard. She looked like she was ready for a morning walk, and I was surprised to see that the weather was quite nice after yesterday's little storm and earthquake. I shrugged, getting ready to head across the courtyard to the lavish grocery store nestled into the Playa Vista Towers complex, but before I could get a chance, I heard the sound of a man grunting like he was struggling to carry something. I turned around to see Tony standing there with his boxes, nearly dropping them all.

"Here, let me help you with those."

"Nah, it's okay, Mia. I got em'," he said right before they started slipping again.

I grabbed the two small ones off the top and that gave him the wiggle room he needed to walk over to the elevator. They were stacked so tall he could barely see where he was going.

"You look like you're working up quite a sweat there, Tony."

"Yeah, well, Kate's been on a mission to get rid of nearly everything I own because they still have Karen's touch all over them. Let's just say back then I left all the damn decorating to her," he murmured with a chuckle.

"Ah, I see. Well I can help you bring these up to your place."

"Nah, nah. You're all dolled up with somewhere to go. I wouldn't wanna take up your time," he said.

"I was just off to the grocery store. Trust me, I can go anytime."

"Alright, if you're sure. Thanks, Mia."

I helped Tony up to the fourteenth floor, watching as he set the boxes down to unlock the door. I was immediately hit with the comforting scent of eucalyptus in the air, following his lead in taking off my shoes before I entered his space.

"Where should I set these down?" I asked.

"Right over there would be fine."

He pointed to the far corner of the living room near the

oversized beige couch that reminded me of my own. I stacked the boxes neatly so they wouldn't fall over, and I rubbed my hands together lightly at a job well done.

"Thank you, Mia. You're a lifesaver."

"It's no problem at all, Tony. I'm just glad to see that things between you and Kate are alright. That night outside the food truck was a little - "

"That night was chock full of surprises, huh?"

"I'll say."

"Hey, if you want to stay, you're welcome to. Kate will be back in a little bit for lunch. I haven't seen you around much lately and I'd like you to join us," he said.

I thought about it for a moment, knowing that this was the perfect opportunity to question Tony about Karen. There was something strange going on with her, stranger than even I could truly understand and I knew I couldn't let this opportunity pass me by.

"That sounds lovely."

"Please, make yourself comfortable. I swear, we never get guests around here anymore. If we do see anybody, it's always at Laura's or Irina's. Would you like something to drink?"

"I get that. Everyone's been trying to find some normalcy I guess. Ah, water would be fine, thank you."

I sat down on the couch, folding my hands in my lap just as he brought over a cool glass of water. He sat across from me with one of his own, and we got to talking about everything. It started as simple pleasantries, trickling down into small talk, and eventually we found the elephant in the room.

"So, everyone's been talking about Jade, huh? Have you heard anything? It's a real damn shame. She was such a gem," he said, and I shook my head.

"Nothing yet. They've got a few new places to look and some people to talk to, but I don't know if anything will really come out of it."

"Oh?"

I bit my lip, remembering every word of what Karen had told me, but for some reason I felt like I could trust Tony with that knowledge. My lips parted and I took him through every detail of what she told me. He didn't look the slightest bit shocked.

"That's Karen. Crazy, psychotic, and she just doesn't know when to stop. The amount of times we were caught in the hallway fighting, I'm sure the guys down in the security room really enjoyed the damn show. I wouldn't be surprised if Karen really did have something to do with Jade's disappearance."

"Think they fought just as much? Maybe there's something on those tapes. Since she was staying here when they were discussing possible business plans."

"It's possible. Good luck trying to find out though. Security in this building is tight. The amount of millionaires that trek through these halls is ridiculous. They're damn good paying customers though."

"Yeah, I'm sure they are."

Security cameras. I need to get a look at them. Maybe there's something on there that could help.

TONY

52 Days Missing

*S*lid the omelette off the hot, sizzling pan, bringing it over to Kate who was spending the entire morning going over documents for her campaign. I barely even saw her anymore, but I knew she was doing some real good shit for Los Angeles. Once she caught a whiff of my fantastic breakfast, she put down her pen and smiled up at me.

"You really are the best, you know," she murmured, and I leaned down to kiss her.

"Anything for my girl. Busy day?"

"Too busy. I have the rally next week, remember? We were going to do everything online, but now since things are loosening up a bit, I may actually get to make a real address," she said, and I could see her eyes light up. They really hadn't done that in a while. Any time she was home she was wrapped up going over documents, writing speeches, tackling government issues. I couldn't even drag her away from her laptop long enough to feed her some damn bolognese.

"You're gonna win 'em all over," I said.

She didn't say a word, reading the document in her hand

ZINA PATEL

like it was the only thing that mattered to her. I sat there for a moment in silence before she eventually looked up at me, raising her eyebrow.

"Huh? Did you say something, honey?"

"Nope. Nothing. Carry on. I better get back to work."

She nodded, not even acknowledging that I cleared the plates, washed up, and managed to sit down for my morning meetings at *Google* before she even got up from her chair. She was so damn distracted lately, I was finding myself wondering where the hell the woman I fell in love with was. *I know she's trying to do some damn good, but that doesn't mean she gets to put our relationship on the goddamn back burner.*

I finished my first meeting of the day, listening to the sound of the Zoom call disconnect when she came over to me, planting a kiss on my lips with her stack of files in hand.

"I'll hopefully be back for dinner. If not, go ahead and eat without me."

"Yeah, okay."

She kissed me again, caressing my cheek with her free hand before rushing out the door. *She really ain't got no idea that we're barely even a couple anymore, huh? How long is this shit gonna go on for?* I asked myself.

I tried not to let it get to me again, because the last thing we needed right about now was another fight. I quickly changed into my gym clothes once my last morning meeting concluded. I slipped on my running shoes, shorts, a grey t-shirt, and popped my AirPods in. Once I got out into the courtyard, I passed the little cafe with the wicker outdoor seating where I'd always see Jade hard at work on her laptop. She'd always have an iced coffee in her hand, her long fingernails maneuvering around her trackpad, and I remembered how many times I'd told her she needed to take a break every once in a while.

Before I met Kate, Jade was the one that caught my attention. She was beautiful, so damn full of life, and to know now that she fucking vanished into thin air made me wonder if my psychotic ex-girlfriend had anything to do with it. *Karen was always jealous of Jade. She wouldn't even let me say two words to the girl without blowing up in my face. Maybe Mia is right. Maybe she finally snapped.*

I couldn't shake the curiosity because I had no idea Karen was trying her hand at having any kind of job, especially not one with that much responsibility. *Just because you're a partier, Karen, doesn't make you a genius at planning them. Hell, I wouldn't want you to work with me either. I know why Jade turned your ass down.*

Seeing that empty spot in the coffee shop patio made me wonder about Karen. I knew that I was probably the only person she'd ever really tell the truth to. *She's been trying to get back in my good graces ever since she realized how serious I am about Kate. Maybe it was all a little too much for her.*

I wasn't the kind of man to pry, but the more I thought about it, the angrier I got because a woman like Jade shouldn't have to go through this shit. I decided that the next time I saw Karen, I'd get the truth out of her. It's been too damn long now that Jade's been missing, and everyone deserves to know what the hell happened.

When I arrived at the gym, I was hit by a gust of cool air from above, and it felt good because outside was fucking scorching. I swiped my card and the receptionist smiled coyly at me. I headed straight for the locker room to put my shit away and chug my pre-workout protein drink. I was ready for a session that would help take some of the edge off, but when I came out with my towel slung over my shoulder, I heard a shrill voice chatting up some trainers over at the treadmills. *Well, what do you know?*

I was going to start with some cardio anyway and I got onto the machine behind Karen who whipped around to look over her shoulder the moment she heard it turn on. *This girl is like a damn piranha.*

"Oh my God, Tony, hi. I didn't expect to see you here. I thought you gave up working out when you got that food truck. Quarantine weight looks good on you, you know," she teased, and I fought the urge to turn right back around to head home.

"Hello, Karen."

"Look, I just wanted to apologize for the way I acted the other night. I guess I'm not exactly on my best behavior whenever I see Kate."

"Right," I said, realizing this was going to be harder than I thought.

"I'd really like to make it up to you. How about we grab juice and an açaí bowl after you're done with your workout? Just two friends grabbing a light snack. I really want to hear all about how Kate's campaign is going," she offered.

I thought about it for a moment, knowing that if I shut her down now she might not ever tell me the truth about what happened between her and Jade. *I guess an overpriced green juice really isn't that much of a sacrifice.*

"Sure. I'll come find you after I'm done. Sound good?"

"Yeah, it definitely does."

She skipped away happily, probably heading for another class in the aerobics room. Her blonde ponytail bounced around as she disappeared behind a corner, and I knew she was probably feeling the excitement of having lunch together. The thought of having to listen to her go on about her day or even talk at all for that matter made my blood boil, but I had to do something to find out what she knows. *Or find out what she did.*

I did my warm-up, headed over to bench press for a new personal best for myself before hitting up the squat rack. Once my workout was over and I was completely drenched in sweat, I made my way back to the locker room to wash up and grab my things. Karen was waiting for me eagerly by the exit and the smile on her face made me think she believed there was still a chance for us. I pressed my lips together, wondering for a moment if I was just wasting my damn time.

We arrived at the juice bar on the other side of the courtyard. Karen grabbed a table with a big red umbrella overhead before anyone else could get to it. She sat down comfortably in one of the bistro chairs, placing her keys down on the wooden table.

"What did you want again?" I asked, trying my best to be polite.

"An açaí bowl. I want extra coconut shavings on the top, please. You're the best, Tony."

I sighed. Inside the ridiculously cold building after waiting in the short line, I placed an order for her açaí bowl and a green power juice, collected them both at the other end of the counter then walked back over to our table.

"Oh my God, yum. I'm starving."

"Is that thing really going to fill you? Shouldn't you be eating real food after a workout?"

"No, silly. Some of us are trying to watch our figures here. Can't be throwing back pounds of pasta every day," she said, spooning some açaí into her mouth.

"You know, Karen, you're not a very nice person."

"I know I can be a bit of a handful, but you used to like that about me, remember?"

"Yeah, well, people change, Karen."

"I still don't understand what you're doing with that conservative girlfriend of yours. I mean, she's so not your type."

"Are we really going to do this again? What happened to two friends grabbing a snack together, huh?"

She glanced down at her açaí bowl, unable to say another word. I watched her expression soften and she smiled calmly at me. We left that conversation behind and talked about all of the supposed party planning she's been doing for the last few months. It was the moment I'd been waiting for, the chance to press her on what she knew about Jade.

"With all the parties happening, you probably wish Jade was still around."

"Why would you say that?"

"Because she was a pretty popular influencer on the rise. Sooner or later people would pay good money for her to even be present at some of these parties," I said.

"You don't think I could've done a good job on my own? You think I *need* someone like Jade to make my job easier?"

"That's not what I said and you know it."

"You might as well have, Tony. As far as I'm concerned, Jade got what she deserved. Maybe if she'd just listened to me in the first place, she wouldn't be in this situation right now. Who knows where the hell she even is," Karen spat.

"Wow. That's a new low even for you. I know what happened between you two, Karen. I know that you were jealous and angry because Jade didn't want you anywhere near her success. Who could blame her? She could be hurt or barely hanging on for dear life right now and you're still taking jabs at her."

"She didn't deserve the success, Tony. She didn't work for it. Some of us have been working for ages trying to get noticed like that."

"Yeah, well at least you had daddy's money to start that little party planning business of yours. That's probably how you even managed to come up with a business plan in the first place."

I could see the true anger in her eyes. Her cheeks were glowing a bright red now, and I knew she was only moments away from slapping me across the face, but I didn't care. I had to keep pushing. I had to find out if my ex-girlfriend was crazy enough to hurt an innocent girl.

"How the fuck do you even know about any of this, Tony?"

She thought about it long and hard for a moment before slamming her neatly manicured hands down on the table.

"That Mia and her big mouth. Ugh. I'm going to kill her."

"I have to ask you, Karen. Did you do something to Jade?"

"What? No! You're so fucked up, Tony. I can't believe I ever wasted my time on you."

I let her go. I wasn't going to get any more out of her now that she was fuming. I sighed, deciding it was time to head back home and prepare for the night ahead. *Let's hope I can at least get some real business down at the pier tonight.*

I was exhausted after a long day of sitting in front of my laptop, listening to the sound of my mouse and keyboard click, while I ran through endless pages of code. I was at least glad that I was taking a night off from the food truck because business was so booming last night that it was worth the time to relax. I took a hot shower, trimmed my damn beard, and picked out a nice shirt because I was taking my lady out for dinner at *The Vine*. It was nearly eight o'clock when I made my way down to the lobby, and as I stepped out of the elevator, I heard my cell phone buzz in my pocket.

I took it out to read the text message from Kate. *I'm so sorry, Tony. I have to take a rain check on our dinner tonight. I know we were both really looking forward to it, but I have to revise my speech. My campaign manager insists. I'll make it up to you. I promise.*

I was tired of all the empty promises. I was tired of busting out new cologne hoping that she'd show up on time for once. I couldn't hide how angry I was this time, and I nearly stormed right back over to the elevator when I heard Aaron's voice behind me.

"Hey, man. You okay?"

"No, not really. Kate and I were supposed to have dinner tonight, but she's been so wrapped up in the campaign I really wonder if there's even an us anymore. I'm fucking tired, man. What are you even doing down here anyway? Waiting on Mia?"

"Nah, she's at Laura's watching some new movie that just came out. Looks like we both got stood up tonight. I was supposed to be meeting a client here, but they're a no-show. I can't tell you how many bad deals I've been dealing with for the past few weeks. It's like no one knows how to do business anymore, you know?"

"Yeah. Looks like we can both use a drink. How bout you come over to my place. We'll grab a beer and watch the game. You even watch football anymore, pretty boy?"

"Yeah, I do. I'll be up in fifteen."

"Yeah, okay."

I was glad I didn't have to spend another damn night alone, waiting up, wondering when the hell Kate was going to waltz through the front door. I heard a knock on my door a short while later, opening it up to find Aaron standing there, undoing his tie.

"How about that beer, huh?"

He looked exhausted. His light brown hair was a mess and that was saying a lot because it was usually perfectly gelled. He had dark circles under his eyes and his five o'clock shadow was coming through. The last time I saw one that bad was when David bust his face open outside my goddamn food truck.

I sauntered over to the fridge to grab two cold ones. I opened them both, handing one over to Aaron, and we clinked our bottlenecks together.

"You hungry?"

"I can't remember the last time I had any real food. It's been five-star restaurants for the last few days and I'm losing it."

"Oh yeah? Sucks to be you. Usually I've got some kinda good food laying around, but all there is in the fridge is yesterday's Thai."

"I'm down."

I warmed it up, handing him a plate, watching him eat like he'd been starving.

"The hell they be feeding you down at those restaurants? Air?"

"Pretty much."

"Damn," I said.

"So, how have you and Kate been?"

"I'll be honest, man. Things aren't good. All that spark we had in our relationship is gone now. All Kate does is work. She doesn't know how to enjoy life anymore. She should be home with me and instead she's campaigning to be mayor. That Eric guy's taken her under his wing, but I don't know how much more of it I can take. I ain't cut out to be dating a politician. It just ain't me."

Aaron nodded, taking a long swig of his beer.

"How have things been with you and Mia? I spoke to her the other day. She's been dealing with a lot since Jade's been gone. After what happened with Karen, I'm surprised there hasn't been a fight yet," I said.

Aaron stared at me blankly and I realized then that he had absolutely no idea. I sighed deeply, telling him every last detail I knew, and he listened so attentively that I couldn't really fight out how he was feeling.

"Mia's really doing everything she can to find Jade, huh?"

"I don't think that girl is going to stop until Jade is safely back home. I can't blame her, but I hope she doesn't get herself in any real trouble."

"Yeah, me, too."

Aaron's expression changed. His jaw tensed, his face hardened, not like he was worried, but like he was angry. I wondered for a moment if I overstepped, but I couldn't see why he'd be that upset.

"You good, man?"

"Yeah. Mia just needs to stay the hell out of this. She's going to end up hurt, and I don't know if I'll be able to fix it then. She can't get involved."

"I'm sure what she's doing is harmless. She's just asking around, trying to put some of the pieces together."

"Yeah, well she needs to stop!" Aaron snapped.

I furrowed my brow at him, putting my hands up, and he slowly calmed himself down.

"I'm sorry. I guess things haven't been the best with us either. This Jade thing is really getting in the way of us."

"I hear you, man. I hear you."

13

MIA

60 Days Missing

*T*wo months. *It has been two months since I last saw you, Jade. I'm no closer to the truth and I really wish you'd reach out again.* I sighed, clutching my cell phone in my hand wishing the screen would illuminate with another text message from her. My hair was starting to fall out of the messy bun it was in, my makeup from earlier in the day had smeared, but I didn't care. I sat up in bed with my laptop on my knees, my fingers clacking away at the keyboard, as I went through every file I'd created on each of my friends. I'd been collecting information, detailing everything I learned, desperately searching for a connection.

I reached over to my bedside table for the carafe filled with water, poured myself a glass, felt the tiredness start to settle in. I had no luck getting into the security room to look at the surveillance footage, and the only person I thought could help me no longer wanted anything to do with this. *I can't be hard on her. Didi could've lost her job, but what am I supposed to do? I need to see those cameras and I need to get back into that damn apartment.*

I dozed off. An hour later and when I woke up, I was

surprised to see that the other side of the bed hadn't been touched. I frantically sat up, grabbed my cell phone, and dialed Aaron's number. He picked up after only two rings and I began to relax.

"Where are you? Do you have any idea what time it is?"

"I'm sorry, Mia. I'm still at Tony's. I'm coming home now."

"Alright."

I hung up the phone and tossed it onto the other side of the bed. I ran my palms over my face out of frustration, wondering why Aaron had even been spending that much time with Tony. The two of them had absolutely nothing in common, but somehow they still spent just about every other night drinking and watching sports. *I wonder what Kate has to say about that. I'm sure she hates it just as much as I do. I barely get to see Aaron as it is and I'm sure with all the work she's been doing on the campaign, she barely gets to see Tony, too.*

I heard the door unlock and shut a little while later. I sat up with my arms folded across my chest. Aaron came into the bedroom and put his watch on the dresser.

"Oh, no. I'm so sorry, Mia. I lost track of time. I thought you'd be fast asleep anyway," he said.

"Yes, well, I woke up and you weren't here. It's nearly four in the morning. God, don't you understand how bad that is? This time two months ago I woke up to find out my best friend went missing, and here you are not even caring enough to let your wife know you're okay."

I practically blew up and, like he always did, Aaron kicked off his shoes and slipped out of his jacket before sliding into bed with me. He kissed the top of my head, hugging me tight, and I began to melt into him.

"I'm sorry."

It sounded genuine, like he felt it deep in his bones, and all I could do was nod.

The next morning I settled in with a piping hot cup of coffee and looked up to see Aaron practically rushing out the door to his first meeting of the day. I barely got a kiss goodbye before his phone started ringing. He slipped his mask over that gorgeous face of his, and just like that, I was alone again.

I opened up my laptop again, scanning over every name in the folder on my desktop, and that's when I settled on Brenda. She was the one that knew just about everyone there was to know in the building. I imagined that had to include some staff who could be easily bribed, or at least I hoped. I pulled out my cell phone, dialing her number.

"Hey, babe. I'm sorry, I'm about to head into a spin class. Can I call you after?"

"Yeah, I was actually hoping we'd meet."

"Sweet. I'll swing by your place after? I was actually supposed to head to the Grove to go pick out a dress for tonight. Restrictions are finally lifting a little. You up for it?"

"Of course I am," I said.

"Cool. See you then."

I hopped in the shower, picking out a comfortable blouse and jeans. I did my makeup quickly, running my fingers through my dark hair that was still holding onto the curls from the day before. I saw the delivery box at the corner of my closet realizing I had a return I had to make. I thought about the last time I was at the mall. Jade had convinced me to buy a pair of patent leather Manolos. I fished them out of the back of my closet, took the lid off the box, and unwrapped the tissue paper. These shoes deserved to be worn.

I slipped them on, thinking of her, hoping that by the end of the day I could figure out how to sneak into that security room unnoticed. *If there's anyone that can help, it's got to be Brenda.* I grabbed my phone, keys, and wallet, slipping them all into my Prada before heading out the door.

∼

Brenda and I arrived at the Grove to see that the place was quite empty. She took me around to a few different stores and I watched as she held up dress after dress, trying to decide which to get.

"What is the occasion, anyway?"

"This new rapper is throwing a party tonight to celebrate moving into the Towers. He's also incredibly hot," she said, and I smiled.

I helped her pick a little black sparkly number that would knock anyone's socks off. We walked through the Grove, enjoying the afternoon sun, when both of our stomachs started rumbling.

"Are restaurants even open now?"

"Patios are, but they need a reservation. I'm sure I can get us in somewhere," she said.

She pulled out her phone, typing away at the screen and before I knew it, she was leading me down to this perfect little seafood spot. When we were seated under the large white umbrella and the waiter finally left with our appetizer order, I had my chance to tell her what she needed to hear.

"Brenda?"

"Hm?"

"Gosh, I don't know how to start. I'm trying to find Jade," I blurted out.

She raised her perfectly trimmed eyebrows at me and that's when I told her every last detail of what I'd learned. She listened closely, her expression blank. I couldn't read it. I wished I knew what she was thinking, because even though she may have been my last hope, I didn't want things to blow up in my face.

"Now that is wild. You think there's something in that apartment that could help find her?" she asked.

"I think it's worth a shot. I can't ask Didi to help again. I also need to see those security cameras because if Jade really was arguing with someone like Karen, it could help me put the pieces together."

She thought about it, sipping on her water just as the waiter brought over our mini crab cakes. She nodded at me with a smile, and I could already tell that she was going to do everything she could to make this work.

"Leave it to me, Mia. We'll get in to see those cameras. I know so many of the security staff that actually do owe me a few favors. The apartment will be a little trickier, but I'll get you in. Let's go find our girl, huh?"

I beamed. It was the first time anyone had been that willing to help me. I was tired of hearing that I needed to get over it, that I needed to let go of Jade altogether. Brenda reignited the hope inside of me that was starting to fizzle out, and for that I was eternally grateful.

I made it home and took a quick nap before unpacking the shopping bags that littered the living room of my apartment. I heard my cell phone buzz on the coffee table and I reached for it quickly, expecting Brenda to have figured something out by now. *It's done. Meet me at midnight. Bring two coke cans.* I stared at my phone screen confused, but I made my way over to my fridge to make sure I had some soda left.

I had been watching the clock all night, waiting around for my phone to buzz again, and when it did, my heart nearly leaped out of my chest. I tore the blanket from my legs, grabbed my tote bag and stuffed the two cans of coke inside. I slipped into my white Oran sandals, tucked my hair behind my ears and rushed down to the lobby. From the moment the elevator door opened, I could smell the delicious scent of warm pizza. When I turned the corner, there Brenda stood with two boxes in her hand.

"Pizza?"

"That's what Brian wanted. One time I needed to get into the security room to delete elevator footage of a wild night with a guy I definitely don't want to remember. It was cheese and pepperoni then, too," she said, and I smiled.

"I brought the soda."

"Good, we're going to need it."

I followed her lead as we walked down the hallway to the back rooms. I could hear the sound of someone tapping on a keyboard and the subtle sighing that probably came with the job. Brenda knocked on the door, and the voice on the other end was very nasal. The door quickly swung open and behind the man dressed in his security gear, I saw the endless amount of monitors. My heartbeat quickened and I imagined there had to be something there that could help me find out the truth.

"Brian."

"Brenda. Is that cheese and pepperoni?"

"Just like you asked. Mia here brought you soda," she said.

I fished the two cold cans out of my tote bag, handed them to him, and his face lit up.

"You have fifteen minutes. Make it quick," he instructed.

Brenda and I both started combing through the security cameras. I settled on a few videos of Jade entering and leaving the building. Every time she turned the corner or was heading in the direction to possibly meet someone, the video would cut. I started searching around trying to find the missing tapes, but they were gone.

"Did you find anything?"

"Someone wiped these, Brenda. There are so many videos missing."

"What about the night Jade disappeared?"

I fast-forwarded to that time, hoping that there would've been something present that we could use. I clicked on the cameras outside the pool bar that evening, and there Jade was chatting with Karen. Her hands were folded across her chest like she really didn't want to be having that conversation, and it only made me wonder how much information Karen was really withholding.

"Well, damn. I had no idea Karen saw Jade the night she disappeared. She certainly left that part out of her story," I murmured.

Brenda and I watched the footage back a few times. Karen stood there in the pixelated video tapping her heels angrily while Jade yelled at her. There was no sound. There was no telling what that could've been about, but now I needed to know more.

~

I curled up in bed that night, squeezing my pillow hard, hoping that Brenda would successfully get us into 1002 eventually. My mind reeled with questions and the more I thought about it, the more I worried that Karen was definitely involved. I wrapped myself in the silk sheets, feeling them brush up against the bare skin of my legs while I attempted to get comfortable. Aaron was out late yet again, but I didn't have it in me to fight about it anymore. *The things he has to do to keep his business afloat. I just wish he'd pay half as much attention to me.*

All of the simple gestures had died down. There were no more takeout dinners and movies on the couch. It was just suits, cocktail parties, and deals to close. None of that involved me anymore, but I wasn't complaining. I had far too much on my mind to worry about helping my husband make more money when we had more than enough as it is.

I had fallen asleep when I heard the soft buzzing of my phone. I reached for it, answering it groggily wondering if Aaron had finally learned to let me know when he was going to be late. I heard nothing on the other end of the line and I pulled the phone from my ear to stare at the number on the screen.

"Oh my God. Jade? Jade, is that you?"

I heard the soft breathing and I knew that there was someone listening to me. I wanted to believe that it was her, I wanted to believe that we could finally put an end to all of this, but she wouldn't speak.

"Jade, please. If you tell me what's going on I can help you. We can fix this, I promise. Whatever trouble you're in, we'll deal with it. Please, talk to me," I begged.

The phone call cut and I felt my heart violently sink into my stomach. I instantly felt like I could cry, but that's when the next text message came through. *You need to stop looking, Mia. If you don't, you're going to get hurt.*

I tossed my cell phone to the other side of the room angrily, feeling it rush through me in a way it never had before. *Why are you playing these games with me, Jade? Why would I get hurt? I don't care what you say. I'm not going to stop looking for you.*

I called the number back a few times, but there was no answer. I wondered if this text message was going to mysteriously disappear too. I was starting to feel like I was going crazy, like the world around me was spinning far too fast and I couldn't get a grip.

I felt like I was suffocating. The sweat started, and I didn't think twice before grabbing my keys and walked out the apartment door. I rode the elevator to the empty rooftop lounge, immediately feeling better once I got a good look at the LA skyline. It was mesmerizing at night. The building lights twinkled, the streetlights were warm, and the sky overhead was so clear I could see the moon.

I took a few deep breaths, allowing myself to relax, and I reached for my cell phone. I fished around in my pockets for it and that's when I realized it wasn't there. *Shit.* The once tranquil moment I was having, dissipated. I felt the cold air on my skin, the sudden feeling like something wasn't right. I glanced over at the skyline once again before I heard it. There was a loud thud behind me, like someone had knocked over a table or chair. I was completely frozen, my breath caught in my throat, and that's when it hit me. *Someone's here. Move. You need to move! Now!*

I rushed to the large wrought-iron door, opening it up as quickly as I could, and I made it back inside. I barreled down the hallway to the elevator, taking the solo ride down to my floor, feeling my heartbeat start to slow. Once I made it back inside I realized Aaron still wasn't home. This time I didn't bother calling him. I didn't bother fighting again. I kicked off my shoes, stripped out of my sweats, and headed straight back to bed.

~

"What do you mean he doesn't want to sign the deal? I can't have that, Howard. The last investment I tried to make didn't exactly work out. I was supposed to be sitting on millions by now. You're supposed to help me make that happen," Aaron barked over the phone.

I sat at our dining room table with him, eating our room service breakfast with its metal tin covers and perfect pads of butter. I glanced over at him to see just how angry he was. I'd never seen him so stressed out, so worked up about something. He banged his fist into the table, knocking over the glass of orange juice next to me. His eyes widened when he realized what he'd done and I stared back at him, waiting for an explanation.

"Aaron, what the hell has gotten into you? You can't blame this on stress, okay? You're never here. When you are, all we do is fight. You fight with the people who work for you. You fight with me. What the hell is going on?" I snapped.

"I can't talk about this with you. You won't understand. You've never worked a day in your life, Mia."

My mouth hung open in shock. I nearly tossed the entire bread basket at him with how much I was fuming. This time the softness didn't return to his face. He didn't rush to apologize like he always had when he said something out of line.

This time he was too far gone to make it right and that's when I began truly worrying about us.

"You can't be serious," I murmured.

"I was on the phone with Mayor Giovanni himself this morning. He's asked to meet with me about some plans for a new shopping district I'm helping to fund. Maybe if you'd spend half of your time worrying about something other than your goddamn friend, you'd understand what I'm going through."

The silence between us was absolutely deafening, and I couldn't believe that we were finally having a fight of this magnitude. Aaron's cell phone started to ring and he took it into his hands, getting up from the table.

"Mia, I love you, but you need to stay out of my business, okay? It's too important."

"Yeah, well I thought we were important, Aaron. I guess I know where your loyalty lies now."

He sighed, shaking his head as he ventured off into his study to take his phone call. I felt the tears rush to the surface of my eyes, and they started streaming down my cheeks before I could stop them. *That's not the man I married. That's not the man I fell in love with.*

I pulled out my cell phone, dialing Kate's number. She's the only person I knew that could help me figure out what Aaron was really up to.

"Hello?"

"Kate, hey. Do you have a minute?"

"Uh, yes. Of course, what's up?"

"I need your help."

14

KATE

61 Days Missing

The new suit I bought was hanging on the valet rod in my closet. It was the perfect cream shade with gold buttons and it matched my Jimmy Choos perfectly. It was the day of the last address I had to give and I finally had some time off. I knew Tony and I were in desperate need of it because our relationship had been hanging on by a thread for the last few weeks. I was worried that he'd eventually have enough of me, leaving me all alone to walk the campaign trail, and that was exactly what I didn't need right now.

I was studying my reflection in the mirror when I got the call. I rushed to answer it thinking it had to be my campaign manager. When I looked down at the screen it was Mia's name and picture. I furrowed my brow. I picked it up. She spoke about Aaron, about his connection to the mayor, and while I promised her that I'd find out what I could, I felt strange about it. *I'm around that man twenty-four-seven and I'm pretty sure he's never met with Aaron once. It's possible they have a clandestine agreement to meet somewhere off the books, but I highly doubt it.*

"I need your help," Mia said.

"I'll see what I can find out. You can come meet me at the Beverly Hills Hotel this evening. I'm giving my address there and we can talk afterwards," I told her.

"Thank you, Kate. You're the best."

Tony was hard at work on his laptop when I came out fully dressed for another day of work at the mayor's office. He seemed distracted. As his meeting was going on, he was texting. He barely even noticed that I was there when I leaned in for a kiss. He pressed his lips against mine quickly before returning to his message and I stood there with my arms crossed.

"What?"

"You haven't said two words to me all morning. What's going on?"

"Nothing. I've just been busy. You've been pretty damn busy yourself," he reminded me.

"Are you coming to my address tonight?"

"Yeah, I'll be there," he said.

I couldn't shake how disinterested he seemed. I was working my ass off to make Los Angeles a better place, to give people a voice. I was working under Mayor Giovanni so I could soon become the first Korean-American mayor, but that all went right over Tony's head. I wasn't the kind of woman that had time to be working tirelessly in the back of his food truck or be home whenever he wanted me to. I had dreams and it hurt that he just didn't seem to care about them anymore.

"I love you," I said, grabbing my bag.

"Love you, too."

He didn't even look up from his keyboard and I tried my best to brush it off, heading down to the lobby with my head held high, but I just couldn't. I missed the people we were before the pandemic hit. We were full of life. Tony loved coming to all of my speeches and press events. I loved being there for him whenever the food truck was booming. That all changed when we were forced to spend so much of our time together, and now I was wondering if we were going to last. *I even risked being cut off by my parents, who warned me not to move in with Tony, and now I had to admit that it may have been a mistake. Living together before marriage was against the rules of my church, and here I am risking it all for Tony, and he doesn't seem to give a damn.*

I was about to head out the automatic doors that led onto the street where my town car was waiting for me, when I heard a shrill voice calling out my name.

"Kate! Kate, wait!"

I tried to walk faster, but my heels still weren't fully broken in yet, so my stride was short and not fast enough to get away from Karen.

"What do you want?"

"Wow, someone's got an attitude this morning. I just wanted to ask what time Tony was bringing his food truck around tomorrow night. I have so many friends that are dying to try his meatballs," she said with a smirk.

It was taking every ounce of self-control not to blow up on her again, but I kept my cool. The last thing I needed was Karen finding out that Tony and I were fighting. *I'm sure she'd jump on the opportunity to get Tony all to herself again. She's tried before and I'm afraid that one day he's just going to give in.*

"Seven o'clock."

"Goodie!"

I rolled my eyes at her. Out into the bright Los Angeles sun, I glanced back for a second to see that she was rather wrapped up in her texting. Her French-manicured fingernails were typing a mile a minute and she had quite the sly smirk on her face. It was almost like she was blushing, and I wondered for a moment if she had somehow rekindled things with Tony. I'd been gone so often that I wouldn't put it past her to try something like that, but now I worried that she was going to steal Tony right out from under me.

She really does have a way of weaseling into everyone's business.

As much as I've tried to keep her away from him, she always manages to get up in his face. Should I be worried?

"Ms. Park?"

I nodded at the chauffeur who held the door open for me. I slid inside, feeling the cool air-conditioning help ease the misery of this heat. I tried not to think about Tony and Karen on my way to City Hall, and as I flipped through my planner, I remembered Mia. I remembered what she'd asked me and how strange it had felt. As I waltzed into Giovanni's carpeted office, I wondered if Aaron really did manage to get the mayor's attention. I waited until he finished up his last phone call, hearing him passionately talk about his children's school board.

When he put the phone down, his entire demeanor changed. He was exhausted, overworked, and looking like he may snap at any minute.

"Kate. Please tell me my day isn't packed with any more appearances. As much as I love children I don't think I can take another round of convincing them all they can be President one day."

"Um, no. I actually just have your speech to approve for tonight. The only appearance you'll have to worry about today is mine," I said with a smile.

I handed him the manila envelope and he pulled out the stack of papers, going over everything I wanted him to say. We were going to cover so many important issues, tackling the pandemic one great decision at a time. Los Angeles had a glimmer of hope this last week because things were finally opening up again, but I'm afraid that was all going to change soon. The cases were rising, the influencers were wreaking havoc at every corner, and we were left to pick up the pieces.

"Did you get a hold of that wacky Instagram girl who threw that ridiculous mansion party? We have to shut that down and remind those rich brats that they're making all of this worse for everyone."

"I got hold of her manager. She's set to make a public apology soon, and she has even agreed to do a PSA," I said.

"That's what I like to hear, Kate. I also wanted to wish you good luck tonight. I know you won't be back for at least a week or two, but I'm damn proud of you. If there's anyone that's set to win this thing when the polls open, it's you. You've got my endorsement."

"What else could I possibly need?"

I smiled brightly, getting ready to leave when the thought of Mia's phone call made me halt by the door. I turned around to see the mayor hard at work on his laptop and he glanced up to see that I was still standing there.

"Is there something else, Kate?"

"I actually wanted to ask you about something, but I'm afraid you're going to think I'm overstepping."

"Oh, please. You're my prodigy. I trust your judgment completely, and you're one of the only people I won't fire for being straight with me. What's on your mind?" he asked, putting his fingers to his lips, waiting for me to get on with it.

"Do you know a man named Aaron Williamson? His wife is a friend of mine and she said that he's been quite involved with helping you look into some investments. I've just never seen you two together before, is all," I said.

The mayor pondered for a moment and I was half expecting him to shut me down, not because he didn't know who Aaron was, but because I was butting into his business. As much as I knew everything there was to know about the Giovanni team, Eric was still a private man who was probably using Aaron to keep his career alive after he was done in office.

"I'm sorry, Kate. I don't know who that is. Trust me, if I did, I'd probably be in a much better position than I'm in. My financial advisor has been looking for that exact sort of thing. Do you think I could get in touch with him?"

"Ah, I'll see what I can do, sir."

He has no idea who Aaron is. Why the hell would Aaron lie to

Mia about something like this? I tried to forget about it, thinking that it had to be some colossal misunderstanding, but I had a bad feeling in the pit of my stomach. *Something's not right here. How am I going to break it to Mia that her husband has been lying to her? If it were me, I'd want her to be honest, too.*

~

I stood at the podium with the bright fluorescent lights shining down on me. The banners and posters with my name on it were plastered around every corner of the Beverly Hills Hotel ballroom. It was a sight to see everyone cheering for me, excited for change, the kind of change that Los Angeles desperately needed. I gave my speech with ease. The balloons and confetti came down around me as Tony leaned in for a kiss. We waved to the crowd one more time before the formalities of the evening were over and the festivities could really begin.

"You did great, Kate. Proud of you," Tony said. I could see him trying to force a smile. I kissed him softly, wrapping my arms around his neck, running my fingers through his hair.

"After tonight, you have me all to yourself. It's time I remind you that I love you unconditionally and that there is absolutely nothing that could ever break us. Okay?"

"I love you, Kate," he said as his face lit up.

"I love you, too."

It was the first time I felt like I got through to him in a while, and watching him mingle with a few of our city council members made me realize that all hope wasn't lost after all. I pressed the wrinkles out of my suit jacket, adjusting the back of my bun slightly, and that's when I got the tap on the shoulder. There Mia was with her beautiful long black tresses flowing down the front of her body, and the blue dress she was wearing was absolutely stunning. *I really should be taking style tips from Mia and Jade, those girls know how to rock an outfit. Whenever Jade turns up, I will offer her the job of official stylist to the next mayor of Los Angeles.*

I saw the look on her face, the one that was practically begging for some sort of explanation. She wanted me to fix what was going on between her and Aaron, to give her a reason for him to be gone all the time. I told myself that he had to be wrapped up in work or that he had another dozen deals to close, but I still couldn't understand why he'd lie to his wife about knowing the mayor personally. *I still don't know for sure if Tony is as faithful as he says he is. One good night doesn't undo a collection of bad ones.* I thought, as Mia handed me a glass of champagne.

"You killed it tonight. Everyone loved you," she said, enthusiastically.

I smiled, flaming out at the small, restricted gathering where no one seemed to get too close to anyone else. Socially distanced or not, it was still a night I was going to remember for the rest of my life.

"Thank you, Mia. That means a lot."

"So, did you find out what Aaron was doing with Giovanni? I mean, I understand if the mayor is the one that's occupying a good chunk of his time nowadays. You can't exactly say no to a man like that. I'm sure you understand. Politicians are quite hard to read, but they know how to get the job done," said Mia.

My eyes darted around the room looking for a way out of this mess. I wished I had a chance to talk to Aaron myself, but it was too late. Mia was here and she was expecting an answer. *Out with it. I'm sure there has to be a logical explanation for all of this, right?*

"I spoke to Eric at the office today and he says he doesn't know Aaron, Mia. I pressed him on it, but he made it clear he has no idea who he is or what he does. I don't know why Aaron would lie to you, but I'm sure there's a reason," I said.

I could see the anger well up behind those beautiful brown

eyes of hers. I was afraid that she was going to jump down my throat or blame me for this. She'd been through a lot over the past few months, dealing with Jade's sudden disappearance, but now I was afraid she was at her limit.

"No. You have to have gotten it wrong. He told me - "

"I'm sorry, Mia. I really am. I think it's time you talk to Aaron about what's really going on here," I smiled sympathetically at her before making my way through the small crowd of people waiting to offer their congratulations.

~

The first morning where I didn't have to roll out of bed at five o'clock to get a workout in before a full day of politics. I relished it, wrapping myself in a satin robe, pulling my hair back in a claw clip so I could fix Tony a real breakfast, his favorite of bacon and eggs over easy, on sourdough toast. I wasn't out of routine yet so I woke up far too early, clanking pots and pans together trying to make it special. By the time he woke up, brushed his teeth, and was sauntering out to the kitchen shirtless, breakfast was already on the table.

"Now, what in the world is this?"

"This is an apology for being such a narcissistic politician who has the best boyfriend in the entire world," I said.

He pulled me in close, his bulging muscles enveloping me in warmth, and I pressed my hands into them as he kissed me. He tucked the single strand of my black hair behind my ear before kissing me again and I was putty in his hands.

"There she is. I've been wondering when you'd show up, Katie," he whispered.

He pulled me away from the eggs, hash browns, bacon and toast, leading me towards the bedroom. We both collapsed onto the messy white cotton sheets and for the first time in far too long, we made love. It was wild, reckless, the kind we had nearly every night when we first got together. By the time we made it back out to the kitchen everything was cold, but I didn't care.

"Leave it to me. You sit," he instructed.

I was still blushing, feeling the heat building between us, which let me know I'd probably be spending the rest of my morning in bed with him until he had to get back to work. We ate breakfast together and I had a quick shower before deciding to treat myself to a massage. I called down to *The Oasis* to book me in right away, and I was pleasantly surprised to find out they had a cancellation. I was on a high from my incredible morning, but on my way out I caught sight of Tony wrapped up in his text messages again. He let out a soft chuckle, tucking his phone away before I got near him.

"Where are you off to?"

"The spa for a massage. I was going to say we should grab dinner tonight but I just remembered you'll be manning the food truck," I said.

"I can fix you dinner and once we close up shop for the night, I can definitely fix you something else," he whispered into my ear, and then kissed me deeply, to remind me of what's to come later.

I left feeling excited but also confused, wondering if I was just reading too much into things. *Maybe I don't really have anything to worry about after all. If I did, I'd be able to tell, right?*

The Oasis waiting room was filled to maximum capacity when I arrived. It seemed that everyone was looking to blow off a little steam. There were a few women clutching their purses, purchasing the latest overpriced skincare at the counter while others desperately waited to get the knots removed from their shoulders and backs. With so many people working from home, hunched over computers and on constant Zoom calls, I guess everyone needed physical therapy. I fell somewhere in the middle of that, locking eyes with the receptionist as soon as I walked in.

"Ms. Park, Derek is ready for you."

"Thank you."

I followed her down the long hallway to my room, listening to the calming spa music, allowing myself to unwind. Once the massage started, my heartbeat slowed and I welcomed the pressure on my back, the scent of the oil lulling me to sleep. It was over far too quickly and when I finally sat up, I called out to Derek.

"Yes, Ms. Park."

"Do you think I can book another one for Friday?"

"Of course. I'll see you then."

His Russian accent was thick, warm, and comforting. I felt incredibly zen. It was like nothing could break how incredible it all was being away from politics, the campaign, and the office, until I heard her voice. Sometimes I forgot that we lived on the same floor, and part of me always thought she got an apartment here to stay close to Tony even after he broke up with her.

Her door was slightly cracked open and I could see that she was moving some large brown boxes out. There were a few pieces from last year's Fall collection, some purses that could get her a pretty penny if she even bothered to sell them online, and some shoes that looked brand new. I didn't want to pry, but I inched closer to the door to see her curled up on the couch, twirling her blonde hair around her fingers, flirting with someone over the phone.

"Well, I have the place all to myself. You can come over whenever you want. I'm definitely in the mood for some good Italian food. How does tonight sound?"

Her voice was low and suggestive like she was practically purring into the phone. The mere mention of Italian food made my blood boil, and I was certain she had to be talking to Tony. My entire body ignited with the kind of fire that was far too hot to tame and I burst into her apartment, grabbing the phone out of her hand to yell at him myself.

"What the fuck is wrong with you, Tony?" I yelled.

"Who?" And then a pause.

From the moment I heard his voice my heart dropped into my stomach. My eyes widened and it was like everything around me was moving in slow motion. *Oh my God. It's not Tony. It's -*

"What the fuck are you doing, Kate?"

She snatched the phone right out of my hand and hung it up quickly, but it was too late. It couldn't undo what I'd just heard. The sound of the voice that didn't belong to Tony, but it did belong to the husband of a dear friend. Suddenly, everything was starting to make sense. The lies he told her, the way he spun the truth, all so he could sneak around with a bitch like Karen.

"I have to tell Mia," I said, heading straight for the door.

Karen ran in front of me, slamming it shut. She looked me right in the eyes and I could see that she had her tail between her legs now. She was going to beg, plead, and cry until I gave in. If that didn't work, she'd probably come up with some kind of elaborate scheme to get revenge on me like she'd tried to do so many times. *My campaign has survived you many times over, Karen. I don't care what you do now. This secret is too big to keep and I would be the last person to ever protect you anyway.*

"You can't tell Mia. This would ruin her. This would ruin everything!"

"You've left me with no choice. When are you going to learn, Karen? There's nothing good about being a homewrecking, psychotic, *bitch*. Now, get the hell out of my way."

15

MIA

63 Days Missing

 $\mathcal{I}$ t was another long day inside. I had the television on, listening to the news report that we were entering the second wave. Life didn't feel too different being in the bubble. Playa Vista Towers was exactly that, a Paradise. The masks, restrictions, curfews, none of it felt as strange as being without Jade for this long. Part of me was starting to wonder if I'd really see her again. I remembered what Karen had said. Uttering those words made me feel like I wanted to vomit, but it had been two long months since anyone had seen or heard from Jade. *What if she's not here anymore? What if it's already too late?*

I tried to snap myself out of it, focus on what I was doing. I knew that no matter what the outcome was going to be, I wanted to know the truth. I needed the truth if I was ever going to have a semblance of a normal life again. I curled up on the couch with my cell phone in my hand, going through my text messages to find any trace that Jade's text had disappeared once again. I sighed, glancing around to make sure that Aaron wasn't looking over my shoulder, and I dialed the one person I promised myself I'd never speak to again.

"Hello?" His voice was low, groggy like he'd just woken up.

It was the middle of the day, but it was a particularly gloomy one. The courtyard was probably empty even though it was usually filled with those trying to soak up the Los Angeles sun. Everybody was looking for the one thing to keep themselves on track whether it would be patio lunches, yoga, or a dip in one of the many pools in the complex.

David wasn't ever the kind of man to get involved with normal activities. When he wasn't working, he was drunk off his ass, ruining the marriage he'd tried so hard to build. Now he was alone. He had no one around him and after the last scene he made, no one wanted anything to do with him.

"I hope this isn't a bad time."

"Not at all, Mia. I'm surprised you're calling me. You're the first person in months that has reached out. Laura has tried, but I know she's only doing that to be nice," he said.

"I'm not calling to check on you, David. I'm calling to ask if there have been any updates about Jade."

I was direct, straight to the point, and I could hear him shift around on his couch like he was looking for the words to say.

"The police haven't found anything. They're convinced she ran away. She took her phone, her keys, even that damn lipstick she wore every day. They dragged my ass through the mud because I had a wife that made a whole damn career online and I didn't even know. I didn't know what she was doing, and now I wished I paid more attention when I had the chance."

It was the first time I could really hear the hurt in his voice. He sniffled and I imagined he was fighting back tears. Everyone else had found it in them to move on, but the two of us were stuck in a time warp, still hoping that Jade would somehow walk right through the front door.

"She couldn't have run away. There has to be something else that they can do."

"There's nothing left, Mia. If I push them too hard I know they're just going to turn the tables around on me. I can't have that. I've been through enough. I've damn near lost everything."

"Well, thank you for letting me know," I murmured.

"Yeah."

I sat there wondering if I'd been wrong. I wondered if I'd been too quick to judge David because the man on the phone sounded like he was desperately searching for answers just as much as I was. *No. That's what he wants you to think. He's the only person that could've hurt her. He'll tell you what you want to hear, but why listen to him? Keep pushing. There's something to find. There has to be.*

I grabbed my laptop, and flipped through my notepad with my daily to-do list, before stuffing it into my Louis Vuitton tote bag. I decided that the only way I'd be able to really clear my head would be to get some writing done. I had nearly two months full of pages, questions, stories that seemingly had no real end. That wasn't going to stop me from searching for the truth, and while I waited on Brenda to contact me about unit 1002, I had some real time to kill.

The courtyard cafe was bustling with the few patio tables they had outside. I snagged the only open one, setting my things down before grabbing an iced matcha latte. I opened up my laptop screen, clicking on the last document I edited before glancing up to see who was sitting at the table next to me.

"Kate?"

"Oh my God. Hi, Mia. What are you doing here?" she asked.

Her eyes darted around the patio and she avoided eye contact with me like she was nervous. I wrinkled my eyebrows at her, knowing that the last time we spoke I didn't exactly get the best news, but it wasn't like I was upset.

"I'm just here to clear my head and get some writing done.

I've been working on a story these past few months. We have been living pretty crazy lives lately, you know."

She smiled awkwardly at me like she wanted to end the conversation right there, but now I was curious. She had a stack of files next to her and some documents in her hand that she had freshly signed. She was so nervous that she knocked her coffee over and it spilled all the way down her navy suit pants. I took all the napkins I had and rushed over to help her, but the documents had been fully soaked now. I wondered what had gotten into her, because she was the last person to ever be this jumpy. Kate could stand before crowds and give amazing speeches off of the top of her head. I've seen her on TV answering tough questions from the media, and she aces it every time. Never have I seen her this rattled. I took the clean seat on the other side of her table and I wasn't going to get up until she told me what was going on.

"Are you okay, Kate? Something has to be on your mind. Is it Tony?"

"At this point, I wish it was."

She gulped hard, her eyes shifting around to see that there were a few people still looking at her after the little accident, but they eventually all went back to enjoying their paninis and mimosas.

"Mia."

"Yes?"

"I don't know how to tell you this and I know I probably should've said something sooner, but I didn't know how to tell you," she began.

"What is it?"

"A few days ago I stormed into Karen's apartment because I heard her flirting on the phone. She left her front door open for all to hear and I was so sure that it was going to be Tony, but when I snatched the phone out of her hand to listen, it wasn't."

"Who was it? Who was she flirting with?"

I sat there waiting for a juicy piece of gossip, something to take my mind off of all the troubles I had for a little while. Though, when Kate's lips parted, I had a feeling I wasn't going to like what she had to say.

"It was Aaron, Mia. Karen and Aaron are having an affair."

I was completely frozen in time. My palms started to sweat, my ears were ringing, and my heart beat so hard in my chest it felt like it was going to burst. There was a tightness I couldn't shake. I clutched onto the handles of the bistro table chair while Kate stared concernedly at me. I shook my head, knowing that my marriage was far from perfect, but I refused to believe Aaron would hurt me like this.

"That's not possible. Aaron would never do that to me."

"I didn't want to believe it either, Mia. It was him. I heard what they were talking about. This is happening," she said.

I could hear the hesitation in her voice like she was worried I'd blow up in front of everyone. I was in such a state of shock that nothing seemed to matter much anymore. I felt absolutely and irrevocably numb. I couldn't say another word to Kate. I stuffed my things into my tote, and stomped straight back to the apartment. I felt the tears well up behind my eyes, the tightness in my throat, and the anger that rushed through me made me want to scream. I wanted to believe that Kate misheard or that she got it wrong, but I trusted her.

Everything came rushing back as the elevator doors opened out onto my floor. The late nights, the fights, the way Aaron had been so distant lately, it all started to make sense now. My cheeks were hot and red with anger. I had no idea where he was, but I pulled out my cell phone as my heels pierced the carpeted hallway. I sent him a text, shutting my eyes for a moment, taking a deep breath. *"I know what you did."*

I opened my eyes just as I heard the stairwell door open, and I saw David moving through as silently as possible, clutching a large brown envelope in his hand. I wrinkled my brow, wondering what that could be about and why he didn't just turn the corner to the elevator where I was. He didn't see me. I was sure of it, but now I wanted to know what the hell he was hiding. As I got closer to the stairwell door, I heard the sound of a feminine voice join him from below with soft clacking of heels following behind. I peeked through the little glass panel to see David standing there with Irina.

My eyes widened and I cracked the door open a bit just so I could hear a bit of their conversation.

"We shouldn't be meeting here."

"This is the only place where people aren't going to ask any damn questions, Irina. They're doing renovations on my floor and you can't seem to get rid of Serge for more than a few minutes. Look, this is important. I found this in the closet hidden in the pocket of Jade's suitcase," said David.

I held my breath afraid that they were going to somehow hear me. I watched David hand Irina a folder, from inside the envelope, and she thumbed through it quickly, reading through the attached documents on the inside.

"Who's the investor? Says here the deal would've made them 6 million dollars. Damn, Jade was about to be one rich bitch before she disappeared, huh?"

"I don't know who it is, Irina. We need to find out and we need to get the cops to look into this shit. They're building their investigation, but I know I'm at the heart of that. I've had enough of this shit. At this point, I don't even care if we get Jade back. I just want this to be over," he murmured, running the palms of his hands over his face.

"This will all be over soon, baby."

I watched her caress David's cheek. Her Manolos were digging into the concrete floor, her beige coat pressing up against him as she leaned in for a kiss. He pulled her in close, running his fingers through her shiny hair, and he kissed her hard. I fixated on the folder in Irina's hand, knowing it wouldn't do me any good anyway if it didn't state who the investor was. There were so many venture capitalists just rolling in cash that lived at Playa Vista Towers, that trying to find out which one Jade had actually thought about signing with would be one hell of a gamble.

I need to find another connection. There has to be something else besides the money that made Jade choose which investor to go with. Jade trusted her gut when it came to people and after what happened with David, I knew she'd choose someone she felt absolutely comfortable with. No amount of money would change that for her. *I can't wait anymore. I need answers now.*

I thought about rushing down the hallway to my apartment to wait for Aaron, but the truth was I really didn't want to see him right now. Instead, I made my way back to the elevator, pressing the button, so I could head down to Brenda's floor. *I'm done waiting. It's go time.*

16

BRENDA

63 Days Missing

$\mathcal{I}$ was wiping last night's makeup off of my eyes when I heard the knock on my door. I washed my face quickly, drying it with a fresh, fluffy white towel before rushing to look through the peephole. Mia was standing there with her arms crossed, her warm skin flushed like she was fuming, and I was immediately concerned. I tied the satin strings of my robe tighter, tossing my hair over my shoulders before I opened the door.

"Mia? Is everything okay?"

"No. It isn't. It really isn't, Brenda. Can I come in?"

I nodded quickly, stepping aside so she could slip past me. I wanted to come right out and tell her that I found a way to get into that apartment. I was waiting until I got the keys before I did, but now it seemed like she was scrambling to get a hold of herself. She looked like she was seconds away from ripping that long, shiny black hair right out of her head.

Mia sat down on my Boucle sofa, tucking her hands into her lap, and I took the armchair across from her. I grabbed the remote on my coffee table to turn off the music that was thumping through my Bluetooth speakers and she glanced up at me with such sadness in her eyes.

"Any word on unit 1002?"

"I was going to call you tonight after I snagged the key from my date. He's a music producer that just started his label, and he just so happens to know one of the investors. He wouldn't give me a name, but he can get me someone who can get us in. We have to keep this between us because if the wrong person finds out, we're screwed," I reminded her.

I was expecting her to start jumping for joy that we were finally getting into that place, but she didn't. She stared right through me like I wasn't even there. I realized then that this wasn't just about Jade. There was something else going on here and it was tearing Mia apart.

"Mia. Sis, what's going on?"

"Hm? Yes. Sorry. I've been so focused on finding Jade lately that I haven't had much time to think about anything else. Like for starters, my marriage is falling apart. Aaron and I were having a few more fights than usual, but I didn't think anything of it. Not until Kate told me that Karen's been having an affair with him," she said, her voice soft and cracking like she was trying to fight back her tears.

"Oh my God."

I couldn't help but furrow my brow and stare at her in utter disbelief. I knew men could be shit, but I had no idea that someone like Aaron was capable of doing something like that. *You know, he has been all over the place lately. I've seen him at every damn party in the building over the last few weeks and he hasn't been with Mia.*

"So, I'm here to ask you if you've heard or seen anything. I don't know what to do or even how to approach him about this. I don't even know if my marriage is salvageable at this point. I can't focus on anything else since she told me, Brenda.

It's like my entire world is spinning out of control," she murmured.

"Mia, I'm so sorry. That bastard. If I see him, I will kill him. Girl, I have to say this: He's been around lately, at just about every party I've been at for a while. I have really thought about saying something to you, I swear, but I was raised to strictly stay out of other people's households. That's a hard rule in the South. But since we're talking about it, I have seen him take his secret phone calls in the corner, but I've never seen him with Karen."

"Yeah, well there's no denying it was her. Kate ripped the phone right out of Karen's hand to find out who she was talking to, thinking it was Tony, but it was my husband instead," she said, dryly.

"Listen, whatever you need me to do, I'll do it. If there's one thing I can't stand it's a goddamn cheater."

"I'll deal with Aaron. I want to see just how much more he's going to lie to me before I tell him what I know. Right now, I need to finish what I started. I need to find out what happened to my best friend."

"Oh, I can help with that."

She shot me a warm, grateful smile. I watched as she sauntered out of my apartment with a look of newly ignited determination in her eyes. *You're one strong girl, Mia. You'll get through this. We're one step closer to finding out the truth, but first, someone needs to put that homewrecking bitch in her place. I'll leave Aaron up to you.*

I took a hot shower, stepping out into my marble bathroom as the steam blanketed the entire space. I pumped some curl cream into my hands, worked it through my hair, and diffused it thoroughly. I tousled it a bit until it fell the way I wanted it to, then made my way over to the walk-in closet to pick out an outfit for the day. I pulled out a trendy little black dress and coat with the perfect heels to match. Once I was dressed, I took one last look in the full length foyer mirror before I left.

I can't get the key until tonight anyway, I thought, thinking of the man that I had spent last night with. His muscles bulging as he had wrapped his arms around me, the scent of his cologne filling my nostrils, the memory left me on a high. He was a man that knew exactly what he wanted, and his connections really didn't hurt either. I smiled, sauntering into the elevator to head down to the lobby. I had a feeling Karen was spending her time hitting up the complex boutiques since we weren't supposed to leave the premises unless it was for essential purchases.

I guess the rules don't really apply to the ultra privileged LA folk, huh? They exist, spend, and thrive all in the damn same place, I thought, clutching my Fendi close to my shoulder as my heels clacked through the marble lobby. I said hello to everyone I passed by, barely making it out the door before someone came over to chat. I spotted the little French boutique at the other end of the courtyard with its menu board-style sign that read: *By appointment only.*

I walked over and the woman at the front entrance took one look at me, glancing down at her iPad, scrolling through the surprisingly long list.

"Name?"

"I don't have an appointment, but I was hoping you'll be able to squeeze me in. My name is Brenda. Brenda Slater. I need an appointment at the same time that Karen Moore has one. Would you be able to have a stylist available for that time? Karen is shopping today, right?" I asked, hoping my hunch was right.

"She's actually in right after lunch. If you come back then, I can handle the appointment myself."

"Thank you so much," I murmured.

Let's hope the clothes are worth it, Karen, because now you have to deal with me.

～

I grabbed a quick lunch at the courtyard cafe while I waited for my appointment. The delicious lobster roll came out on a perfectly toasted brioche bun and a side of fries with a garlic aioli accompaniment. My stomach growled as I dug in, scrolling through my social media, and sending out a few tweets. I had so much work left to do on my app update, but I promised myself that after tonight, I'd work straight through the next few days. *Right now my friends need me. Especially Mia. When we get into that apartment, I hope she finds what she's looking for.*

Part of me worried that it was just going to be another colossal disappointment. I'd been following the investigation closely and after not hearing so much as a word about what the police were really doing, I felt like they swept Jade under the rug. *I guess money really doesn't buy everything, huh? The entire world can love you one minute, and the next they're scrolling past articles about you like you didn't even exist.*

I blotted my lips with the paper napkin and fixed my lipstick before heading back to the boutique. The stylist started pulling things for me while I sat comfortably on the tufted lounge chair near the dressing room. Only two clients were allowed in at a time. Like clockwork, Karen burst right through the door exactly ten minutes late, clutching her Chanel close to her chest.

"Oh my God, Eleanor, I'm so sorry I'm late. I got a little caught up," she said.

I got a good look at her before she even realized that I was sitting here. She looked disheveled, her lipstick was smudged, and I noticed the desperate attempt to blend out her bottom lash line mascara. *God. In the middle of the day? Really? While Mia is probably off somewhere wondering where the hell her husband is? Disgusting.*

The stylist with her black fitted blazer and gold lapel buttons came back over with an arm full of clothes. She was about to lead me into my private dressing room before I stopped her.

"Would you actually mind if I browsed a bit before I started trying things on?"

"Of course, Brenda. I'll be here if you need me. Just shout," she said, and I smiled.

"Thank you."

I waltzed over to the clothing rack at the front of the store, looking through a few dresses until Karen spotted me. She tapped me lightly on the shoulder.

"Oh my God! Brenda! I didn't expect to see you here," she said.

"Just doing a little shopping. I'm surprised you have time to shop with all of the extra curricular activities you've had lately."

"What do you mean?"

"I don't understand how someone could ruin someone else's marriage and not feel the slightest bit bad about it. That's where you were, right? Screwing Aaron?"

The look of shock on her face wasn't enough to put out the fire inside me. I was fuming in a way that I hadn't in a long time, but I knew it was no match for what Mia was going through.

"I-I don't know what you're talking about," she murmured.

"Right. Don't play dumb with me, Karen. There's a reason that no one around here likes you. There's a reason why Tony dumped your ass when he had enough of you being bat-shit crazy. Don't think Aaron won't do the same thing once he's done with you. He's scum for cheating on Mia, but so are you," I spat.

"You have no idea what I've been through, okay? Aaron was just - "

"Aaron was just what? He's someone else's husband. Though, I know you like to sleep with married men and chase men that aren't yours. It's your speciality, isn't it? You have quite the reputation around here, Karen. Maybe it's time all of your fancy friends know exactly the kind of person you really are."

I pulled out my cell phone, my cheeks grew hotter by the minute, and I started typing the biggest tweet blast I'd ever put out. Karen tried to snatch the phone out of my hand, but I wasn't going to let her. I pressed the button to put my phone to sleep when I was done, and I smirked at her, watching her mouth hang open in shock.

"What the hell did you just do?"

"Payback's a bitch. Good luck getting into any parties now, Karen. It's still not enough to make up for what you did, but it's a start."

"Ugh!"

She huffed and puffed and stormed right out of the boutique forgetting that she had two designer blouses in her hand. She tried to push past the store clerk, but the sensors went off, and she asked that Karen follow her to the back. We locked eyes one last time before the door shut, and I was filled with a sense of victory I knew would last for quite a while.

I slipped into my best silky red mini-dress. I fastened my gold diamond tennis necklace, watching it sparkle as I reached for my Louboutins. My hair bounced in perfect curls while I reached for my purse, slipped my phone inside, ready to see him again. *Don't let him get under your skin. You know these music producer types. They're all game.*

I heard my cell phone buzz right as I was about to head out the door, and I checked it quickly to see the text message that made my heart flutter. *I'm here.* I sauntered down the hallway, pressing the elevator button, hearing it ding! immediately. I entered the library bar, inhaling the scent of cologne wafting through the air. I saw him sitting in a grosgrain leather chair, looking as handsome as ever.

"Brenda, you look absolutely gorgeous, woman," he said, his voice warm, making the butterflies in my stomach run wild.

He kissed me lightly on the cheek and I took the seat across from him just as a waiter came around to take our drink orders.

"A dirty martini, please," I said.

"Scotch for me, thanks."

The waiter walked off, leaving me alone with William, and I couldn't stop the smile from surfacing whenever I looked over at him.

"I had a nice long chat with my friend who will be meeting you in an hour. He'll take you up to the unit. Apparently, no one lives there. If you're looking to move, I'd say it's a great spot. Lots of natural light," he said.

"How do you know?"

"I saw pictures of the old listing. Now I get why you want it so badly."

If only you knew why I really wanted to get in there, I thought.

"How did you convince your friend to do this? This friend, your *investor* friend who has a lot of connections in this building," I teased.

"Oh, Brenda. He's not an investor. He owns the place in full."

I stared at him shocked, tilting my head to the side, completely impressed by his level of networking. I never thought I'd see the day where I'd meet someone that completely outdid me in that department.

"Wow. It must be good to be you."

"Oh, it definitely is," he murmured, with a wink.

"So, how exactly is this going down?" I asked, curiously.

"I called in a favor with the owner. I told him I was scouting places to hold a release party. He said it was alright. I'll have one of the staff meet you afterwards so you can grab the key. Sound good?"

"Sounds perfect."

I felt his hand lightly brush against mine, his fingertips soft and warm, making me practically melt into him. If it were up to me, I'd take him right back up to my apartment for another night of wild sex, but I had a plan and right now, I had to follow through.

Our little rendezvous ended with another drink and a small appetizer. I grabbed my purse, getting ready to head out when he wrapped his hand around my wrist, holding me back for a moment.

"When will I see you again?" he asked, his voice so soft it was practically a whisper.

"Whenever you want, Will," I responded, with a wink.

I caught sight of that dashing smile and those perfect pearly whites before I made my way back into the lobby, looking for this friend of his.

"Excuse me, are you Brenda?" I heard a voice from behind me ask.

"Yes I am."

He reached into the pocket of his vest, pulling out a small white envelope with a small bulge in it, pressing up against the sides. He glanced around once quickly before handing it to me, and I nodded.

"Have this back to me within the hour. It can't be gone long or we're all going to be in a whole lot of trouble," he said.

"Thank you, uh, Mark." I read his little gold name tag, realizing that he was part of the building's staff. Part of me still wondered how William managed to pull something like this off, but I was glad. I pulled out my cell phone and dialed Mia's number, hoping this little bit of news would cheer her up a little.

"Hello?"

"Mia, I got it. Meet me there. We only have about forty-five minutes to get this done," I said.

"I'll be there."

Her voice was quivering and I could tell she was probably crying and exhausted after the day she had. She sounded unsteady with a semblance of worry and a whole lot of frustration. I wish I knew how else I could help her. *I know she's looking for a distraction right now, but she needs to talk to Aaron. That's the only way she'll know for sure what needs to happen.*

~

I made it up to the tenth floor, taking a quick glance down the hall to make sure there wasn't anyone lurking. I felt the nervousness creep up on me nearly out of nowhere. The elevator *dinged!* again, opening up to reveal a tired Mia, clutching the sleeves of her sweats to her chest. My heart nearly leaped right out of my chest.

"Are you ready for this?" I asked, the words leaving my lips before I could stop them.

"I honestly don't know. I've been waiting for this moment forever. I hope there's something in here that could lead me to Jade. I had all of five seconds before someone showed up last time. Didi got spooked, and I believe she still is. I just want answers. That's the only thing that could make me feel the slightest bit better right now."

I nodded, turning the key in the lock, opening the door, fumbling for the light switch. When I got it, I looked out into the empty room. It was a big blank slate with a clean kitchen, perfect cream walls, and sheer window treatments over the floor-to-ceiling windows. I glanced behind me to see Mia standing there with a look of shock I didn't expect.

"No. No, this isn't possible. Brenda, this isn't possible!"

"What? What isn't possible?"

"The place is cleared out. The last time I was here it had

furniture, filming equipment, some of Jade's things. It was littered with her stuff everywhere and now it's all gone," she said, the tears starting to stream down her face.

"That doesn't make any sense."

"Someone knows I was here. Someone knows I'm getting close, Brenda. Now, I may never know. I may never know what happened to Jade."

17

MIA

70 Days Missing

𝒩 *othing seems to make sense anymore.* I walked through the empty apartment, trying to remember what it looked like when it was full. I stepped into the place where the couch had been, the coffee table, the rack of unworn clothes. It was like all that was left of Jade had been stripped away, and it made my stomach turn. I wondered deeply about how things could've possibly gotten this bad. I wiped away the tears that were exposing my bare skin, the tissue in my hand stained with foundation.

I turned to look at Brenda who had been glancing around, probably trying to make sense of this ridiculous mess we were in.

"Thank you Brenda for everything you did. I know it wasn't easy getting a hold of this," I said, waving the key at her.

"It's my pleasure, Mia. I just wish there was something here to find."

"Me, too."

I walked through the guest bedroom, the study, and finally the master. I stepped into the large, empty walk-in closet that had nothing but a few wooden hangers inside. I turned around to head right back out the door when the heel of my shoe got caught on something. I picked up a crumpled takeout menu, opening it up to see that it was for Natalee Thai, the place I loved that was a good thirty minutes away from home.

I turned it over to see a number on it written in sharpie. I read it out carefully, realizing that the person who had written it was me. I remembered pulling the sharpie out of the kitchen drawer, scribbling the number for the event planner down on the takeout menu when I was planning my anniversary party. Aaron had folded that menu card, slipping it into the pocket of his wallet, where I'd seen it only just a few weeks ago when he told me to grab cash for pizza. My heart sank, my palms grew sweaty all over again, and that's when it hit me. The only person I never suspected was my husband. In the span of just a few hours I learned about who he really was. He was a liar, a cheater, and now I knew he could've very well been responsible for the disappearance of my best friend.

"Did you find anything?" I heard Brenda call out from the living room.

I quickly slipped the takeout menu into the pocket of my sweatpants before heading back out to her.

"No, nothing." I had to figure out what the hell was happening before I could possibly share this. *Is Aaron somehow responsible? Ohmigosh, this day can not get worse.*

Brenda looked at me sympathetically and as she took the key from me, I tried not to look her in the eye because I knew if I did, I'd burst out in tears. I didn't want her to know what I'd just found. I didn't want anyone to know until I was sure I had all the facts.

"I'm so sorry, Mia. Is there anything else I can do?"

"No, Brenda. Thank you. I'll figure something out. I know I will."

She smiled softly at me, and reached out to give me a quick hug, before we both parted ways and I headed back to my apartment. I was all ready to confront Aaron about what he'd done, but now I was scared. I was scared that the man I married could've very well been the one to do something terrible to Jade. I was scared that once I jumped down his throat about what he'd done, he'd hurt me. It was once, a very long time ago, and not directed at me, but I have seen a side of my husband when he loses his cool, and when he is filled with rage, he can be scary. I pulled my cell phone out of my pocket to look at the text I sent him earlier. *It's too late now, isn't it? He has to come clean.*

My heart was beating rapidly when I unlocked my front door, and even though all of the lights were off, I knew that Aaron was there. He was sitting on the couch at the far corner of the room, clutching a glass of whiskey closely.

"Where were you?"

"You have no right to ask me that after what you've done," I said.

I was shaking hard. I grabbed the sleeves of my sweater, trying to stop myself, but I couldn't. As I stared deep into Aaron's eyes, it was like I was looking at a complete stranger.

"What exactly do you think I've done?"

"You're sleeping with Karen!" I shouted at him. I had wanted to keep calm, but I lost it. "After everything we've been through together, you threw it all away for some meaningless sex with that crazy bitch?"

"Who in the world told you I was sleeping with Karen? Come on, Mia. You know me better than that. You know that I would never hurt you like that. Whatever sick, twisted lie Karen came up with to further her own fucking agenda, that's on her. I'm not going to let her ruin our marriage because she's known to cause chaos," he said.

I was surprised at how genuine and how calm he sounded. If I hadn't found that menu laying on the floor of unit 1002, I probably would've believed him.

"Kate heard your voice on Karen's phone when she took it from her thinking it was Tony!" I yelled.

"Right, so Kate heard my voice on the other end of Karen's phone. Karen is notorious for what exactly? That's right, flirting and making a fool out of herself. One of my business associates wanted a hot blonde chick to take out to dinner and I suggested Karen, since she'd be much better off staying away from Tony. Isn't that what Kate wants anyway?"

He made me feel so foolish and it shocked me just how effortless it was to find an answer for every question I had. He had a reason to explain every doubt and I knew that if he really was as dirty as I thought, I'd have to do a lot more to find out the truth.

"Y-Yes, I guess."

"Mia, I think this whole Jade thing is driving you a little crazy. Look, I would never hurt you that way. I love you, I love you so much," he said, waving for me to join him.

I reluctantly obeyed, sliding into his arms, feeling the folded takeout menu burning a hole in the pocket of my sweatpants.

"I-I'm sorry, Aaron. I love you, too."

The words hurt falling from my mouth and I tried my best not to flinch as he brushed the hair out of my face, kissing the top of my head.

"It's okay, babe. It's okay."

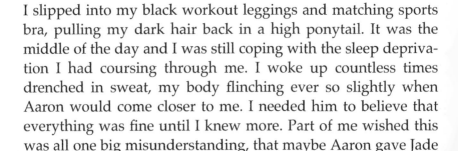

I slipped into my black workout leggings and matching sports bra, pulling my dark hair back in a high ponytail. It was the middle of the day and I was still coping with the sleep deprivation I had coursing through me. I woke up countless times drenched in sweat, my body flinching ever so slightly when Aaron would come closer to me. I needed him to believe that everything was fine until I knew more. Part of me wished this was all one big misunderstanding, that maybe Aaron gave Jade that takeout menu somehow as a friendly gesture, but I felt sick to my stomach about it.

Am I going crazy? I know Aaron. We've been married for three years. He's seen me at my worst and at my best. He consoled me whenever I got another negative pregnancy test when we were desperately trying to start a family. Could he really have been the one to hurt Jade?

I was tired of the questions taking up space in my mind and I needed to blow off some steam, so I went down to the gym. I could hear the sound of weights hitting the platforms, the treadmills running, and the top-forty pop music playing over the speakers. I quickly tucked all of my things into an empty gym locker, stuck my AirPods in my ears and I started my warm-up.

I headed for the treadmill, stepping on and slipping my water bottle into the cup holder. I started off slow, stretching my arms a bit. Through the music thumping directly in my ears, I heard the muffled sound of someone calling my name. I looked to my left to see Jordan standing there with his sleeve of tattoos and impressive muscles. He was sweating from head to toe, his skin flushed like he'd been putting in the work, and he shot me a friendly smile. Jordan was not exactly my typical type, but there was something so attractive about him. Normally I tried to suppress those feelings but today, with all of my new doubts about Aaron, I decided to let my mind wander. Fantasizing about him would make treadmill time fly by.

"I don't think I've ever seen you down here before, Mia. Trust me, I'm here every day," he said, wiping his sweat off with a towel.

"I heard it's good to blow off some steam in a place like this. Aaron seems to love it. I decided to see what all the fuss was about," I said.

He nodded, and that's when I remembered that they work out together. I thought about when Aaron would have some semblance of free time and he'd rush to meet Jordan for a gym session. *You probably see my husband more than I do, Jordan.*

"Yeah, man, we used to get some real good sessions in before he changed his damn schedule. We had a good thing going, working out at seven in the evening every day after work. It was good. One day he woke up and decided to become a damn morning person," said Jordan.

"What do you mean?"

"He works out at four in the morning now. It's crazy. I've been trying to get on his level lately. I'm sure you know, the man's got one hell of a pump." He flexed his muscles at me, pointing to his biceps, and I raised my eyebrow, nodding.

"I didn't know he changed his gym time. I guess it's because I'm usually always fast asleep then."

"Yeah, well I've been doing good these past few days. I've been meeting him nearly every morning. Hey, is he good? Lately he's been a little out of it. Yesterday morning he nearly walked straight into the squat rack."

"No kidding," I said, waiting for him to tell me more.

"He's usually the one telling me I need to get my shit together."

"He's been really busy with work lately or so it seems. I noticed he's been really distracted too. Has he said anything?" I asked.

Jordan stood there with his arms crossed, thinking about it for a moment, but he shook his head.

"No, I was hoping you'd know what was going on. Can't have my gym bro missing a spot or something, you know?"

I have no idea what that means, I thought, but I nodded, smiling at him before one of the trainers called out his name. He bid me goodbye, rushing off to talk to her, and it seemed like they were really hitting things off. She had a smile that lit up the room. She was also in the best shape I'd ever seen anyone in, and it made me wonder how much time people really spend here.

I finished an hour on the treadmill while watching a repeat episode of Wendy Williams, and was getting ready to get off with my slightly wobbly legs when Jordan came back over to me.

"Hey, Mia. They're giving out free sandwiches upstairs for some workout event. Wanna grab one?"

I glanced behind him to see that the blonde he was talking to earlier was wrapping her arms around another trainer, pulling him in close for a kiss. *Ah. So that didn't work out, huh? Need a friend to soften the blow. Maybe I can push him for a little more information.*

"Sure. That sounds great."

I followed him up the stairs, feeling the sweat really start to sink into my workout gear. We lined up to get our sandwiches. I got smoked salmon on whole wheat, which hit the spot after my workout. Jordan and I grabbed a table outside on the patio, and he scarfed down his entire sandwich in minutes, even before I had the chance to take a bite of my own.

"Jordan, has Aaron been getting any weird calls lately during his workouts?"

"Ah, why?"

"He's got this client that's been stressing him out. I just want to make sure that isn't the reason he's been so distant," I lied.

"Actually, come to think of it, his phone has been blowing up. I used to think it was real weird for him to get that many calls that early in the morning."

"Do you know who it is? He'd kill me if he found out I even wanted to meddle in this, but I can't help myself. Maybe if I could just have a word with them I could find a way to fix things," I said.

"I don't know who it is, but I'm sure I can find out. If it'll help, of course. Don't wanna see my bro down like that, you know?"

"Yeah, thank you, Jordan. Also, it would be best to keep this between us. I don't want him getting even more stressed out."

"Noted. Your secret's safe with me."

~

I sat at the dining room table with my laptop open, the soft warm lighting overhead, and I looked over to get a glimpse of the Los Angeles skyline. It was beautiful, absolutely peaceful, but it couldn't take away the pain I felt inside. The more I learned about Aaron, the more I realized that I didn't know him at all. I opened up the document I'd been writing in, staring at the words I finally managed to string together in a story that still lacked an ending.

Every unseen twist and unanswered question was sitting in that document. It made me think of every strange thing that has happened since Jade went missing. The apartment was empty, the takeout menu from Aaron's wallet the only thing that remained. I got two text messages supposedly from Jade only to find that they were deleted the next time I went scrolling for them. *Aaron is the only person that could've deleted them, but why? What does he have to hide?*

I sipped on my lukewarm tea, thinking about how he always seemed to have a perfect excuse. He wrote off the Karen thing as me just being crazy, he told me that I was the one on the verge of losing my mind, but I couldn't possibly trust him. I knew that there was something sick going on here. I could practically feel it, but I needed answers. I needed the truth.

I shut my laptop screen, hearing my cell phone ringing, and I nearly leaped right out of my chair. *Oh my God. Brenda.*

"Hello?"

"Hi, Mia. I was just calling to check in on you. I know it's been a few days since everything went down. I'm sorry again about what you're going through," she said.

"No, it's okay, Brenda. Aaron told me that there's nothing

going on between them. He said that he was actually trying to set her up with one of his associates and she was flirting with him, as she does."

"Ah, Mia, I don't think that's true. See, I confronted Karen about everything. This wasn't just stirring up drama. She did this, and she's probably still doing it. She didn't deny it once. I threatened to put her on blast and she begged me not to. If she had nothing to hide, she wouldn't have acted that way. I really think there's something going on between them," said Brenda.

"Thank you, Brenda. I appreciate you looking out for me."

It was enough to enrage me again. The fear started to melt away and it was replaced by the feeling of utter betrayal. It was enough to get me on my feet so I could start searching through Aaron's things because I knew he had something to hide. *Knowing you, you'd probably keep things right under my nose because you thought I was too stupid to look for myself. You can't talk your way out of this one especially if I find something, Aaron.*

I started going through the nightstands, finding nothing but some business books, hand cream and his watch. I made my way to the closet, searching behind his clothes in the boxes and dust bags on the shelves, but there was nothing. I sighed, running my fingers through my hair, pulling it up into a high bun so I could continue searching without my hair bugging me. I looked through every corner of the study, but there were no locked drawers or hidden spaces where he could've stashed anything. I tapped my foot on the wood to see if there were any loose floorboards, but it didn't help.

There has to be something around here somewhere. I thought. I glanced back over to our master bedroom, realizing the only other place left to check was the en-suite. I remembered the early mornings when we first got married, how he always took out his clippers in their carrying case which he stashed under the sink. It was how he kept that perfect beard of his neatly-trimmed, and it made my heart hurt to know the happiness we once felt was now gone.

I almost didn't even bother to look in there because the thought of him stashing some damning evidence in his clippers case seemed too good to be true. I decided to look anyway, going through the entire thing only to find that there was nothing there. Though, when I went to put it back I noticed that there was an old box from when I'd purchased some Jo Malone candles for the house. I thought I'd thrown it out ages ago, but when I took it into my hands and shook it, something moved inside.

I opened up the lid to find that there were a few Polaroid pictures and an old camera. I turned them around to see that there were some pictures of Karen in lingerie. Some were her sprawled out on the bed, others were where she was fully naked. I went through the stack to find one of her kissing Aaron, and I realized this was what they got up to after all. My stomach turned at the thought of them together, that I nearly believed all of Aaron's calculated lies. *You sick fuck.* I thought.

The only other thing in the box was something wrapped in a light beige cloth. I opened it up slowly, my mouth hanging open once I realized what it was. I held it carefully on the bed of fabric, staring down at the engagement ring with a crusted dark substance on it. *Is that blood? Oh my God. This is Jade's ring. Why does Aaron have Jade's ring? No. Oh my God. No.*

I felt all of the food I'd eaten earlier start to resurface and I dropped the ring back into the box, heading over to the toilet to vomit. *He did this. I was looking for answers this entire time and they've been right here, right under my nose. I can't confront him yet. I need more. Who the hell are you, Aaron?*

18

JORDAN

72 Days Missing

J grabbed the bags of frozen fruit from the freezer and
tossed some into the blender on my kitchen counter. I
dumped two scoops of protein powder in there because I
needed a real pump today. I heard the soft meowing coming
from my living room and before I knew it, my cat Bella was
zooming around the entire apartment.

"Hey, hey. What's all the fuss about?" I asked her the
moment she stopped.

I ran the blender, pouring out my smoothie into a glass
before taking it to the couch. I downed it fast, feeling the brain
freeze hit me hard and settle. My Labrador came rushing over
to me, curling up under my feet for a nap. It was a peaceful
morning, and I was starting to get accustomed to waking up
this damn early. It was still dark outside when I grabbed my
keys and went down to the gym. When I got into the elevator, a
hot brunette came in right after me.

She was wearing tight green leggings and a pink sports bra.
She reached over to press the button to the gym and I took a
quick peek at her ass. *Damn.* I thought, smiling to myself.

"Early morning workout?"

"Yeah, it's the only time I have to work out when I'm not working," she said.

Her voice was soft, sexy, and I just imagined what it would sound like saying my name.

"What do you do?"

"I'm a lawyer."

"Criminal or Corporate?"

She turned around to face me, her arms crossed over her chest, and the look in her eyes made me think I was just about to get a lecture. Though, she just laughed, and I got a good look at that cute little dimple of hers.

"What makes you think it's any of those?"

"Just a hunch."

"Well, if you must know, it's Criminal."

"See, I knew I was right," I teased.

She giggled just as the elevator doors opened and we both stepped out into the small gym. It was a secluded one in the building that was by appointment, which I usually preferred over the more public one across the courtyard. *I'm never in the mood to make that walk when it's so damn cold out at this hour.*

"So, are you going to tell me your name?" she asked.

"It's Jordan. Yours?"

"Addison."

"Nice to meet you, Addison."

We got to talking and an entire half hour passed me by before I realized that Aaron was late. I thought that was strange because he was always the one that jumped down my throat about missing sessions. I checked my cell phone quickly to see if he texted, but he didn't. *Maybe he just overslept.*

Addison was telling me all about life living in Playa Vista Towers as a criminal lawyer. The world around us has changed so much in the span of just a few months, it was cool to see how others managed to adapt.

"Can't be so bad working from home in this little paradise of ours, you know?"

"I mean, it's not all good. You heard about the girl that disappeared, right?"

"Yeah, she's a friend of mine," I said.

This seemed to intrigue her because she started asking me all kinds of questions to the point where I was wondering if we'd ever get to work out at all.

"Look, uh I really don't know what happened to her. We all haven't heard anything and the cops don't seem to have any leads," I murmured, shifting around in my seat on the bench.

"What do you think happened?"

"Who knows?"

She was about to say something else before she looked past me to the entrance and I turned around to see Aaron standing there clutching his gym bag. She seemed to blush when she saw him, twirling her hair like she was far more interested in him than me.

"Looks like you got yourself a new workout buddy," said Aaron.

"No, no. That spot's still reserved for you." I rolled my eyes playfully at him. He seemed to be in a much better mood today and I wondered why. Addison started flirting with him and I knew I had to break things up otherwise we'd have to leave here without so much as breaking a sweat.

"Addison, Aaron and I really need to get to our session. Hate to break up this little love fest here, but he really needs to get back home to his wife," I said.

Her eyes widened and Aaron laughed.

"Nice meeting you, Addison."

We parted ways and I glanced behind me to see her scoffing as she walked off.

"What is it with you and women? They all just flock to you, even the ones that were supposedly interested in me five minutes ago."

"They just like my charm. Maybe you need to work on that one, bud," he said, tapping my shoulder.

"Yeah, yeah."

The workout was exactly what I needed. It was the start to my day that felt right, but I couldn't help but be distracted by Aaron's phone going off every few minutes. He had to grab it from the bench to turn off the sound eventually because he was getting so many notifications. *Damn. I knew he was a busy man, but that's a whole new level on its own.*

I went to grab my water bottle when I saw his phone screen light up again. I glanced down to see Serge's name pop up. Once the call stopped, I noticed that Serge called at least three times. I thought it was strange, but I didn't say anything to Aaron. He was too busy doing bicep curls in front of the large mirror. I patted my face dry with a fresh towel just as Aaron and I got ready to part ways.

"Now I see why you're in here this early. If people be blowing up your phone at this hour, I can't imagine what would happen when the rest of the world wakes up," I said.

"Yeah, well, I guess business never sleeps, huh?"

"I guess. You gotta take a break every once in a while, bro. Shit's not good for you to be operating at full speed all of the time. I see why Mia's so worried about you."

"Mia?"

"Yeah, she's been asking questions about you. She noticed how stressed out you've been lately. When I told her you're working out with me at four in the morning, she looked real shocked."

"I told her so many times, but she always seems to forget. She's been a little out of it. We've been trying to work through some stuff. This whole thing with Jade's got her going a little crazy. Did she talk to you about that?"

"Uh, no she didn't. Why?"

The look on his face quickly changed and I noticed that he seemed immediately interested in what I had to say. It felt weird, but I brushed it off, telling myself that it was too damn early for this. *We're both probably a little sleep deprived. That's all.*

"Oh, no reason."

"I heard she's been talking to everyone else though. I mean, it's fucked up, isn't it? She just disappears out of thin air and even the damn police can't find her? David doesn't seem to have much to say about it either."

"I don't really want to talk about Jade, Jordan. I hear it enough from Mia," he snapped.

"Uh, okay. I mean, I know you and David used to be really close so - "

"So what? I said I didn't want to talk about it anymore. Will you just drop it?"

"Yeah. Yeah, sure."

He stormed off without another word. I felt a weird feeling in the pit of my stomach like something wasn't right, but I couldn't quite put my finger on it. I shrugged, thinking that Aaron just had his goddamn panties in a bunch because he was stressed out.

That's what Mia said, isn't it? I guess there's trouble in Paradise after all. Mia and Aaron were everyone's favorite couple. What the hell happened to them?

~

I spent the afternoon answering emails at the courtyard cafe, getting some work done, and drinking their ridiculously over-priced espresso. Once I packed up, heading through the lobby to the elevators, I spotted Mia checking her mailbox. It was then I remembered that she asked me to call her. *Shit. I completely forgot about the Aaron thing.*

"Mia!"

"Jordan, hey," she said, tucking her mail into her purse.

"I'm so sorry I forgot to call you. Listen, I don't know who can account for the other dozens of notifications Aaron gets, but I did see Serge's name pop up a few times. I don't know if they're doing business together or not, but I thought it was a little weird."

"Serge called Aaron at four in the morning?"

"Five actually. We had a little late start to the session, but he was especially snappy today."

"How so?" she asked.

I could practically see the curiosity on her face. She stared at me blankly waiting for an answer, and it was then I caught sight of just how nervous she seemed. I furrowed my brow, trying not to get in the middle of their marriage shit because it really wasn't my place, but I couldn't just lie to her.

"He brought up you and the Jade thing. I barely said two words about it, but he completely blew up. Any idea why that might be?"

Mia shrugged, pressing her lips together like she really didn't want to get into the middle of this with me.

"No clue. Thank you, Jordan."

19

MIA

75 Days Missing

$\mathcal{I}$ sat in my favorite seat at the library bar clutching my purse as I sipped on my martini. I checked my phone screen countless times hoping that he got my message loud and clear. I heard footsteps approaching from the entrance and I turned around to see Serge standing there in one of his expensive suit jackets. His hair was a clear silvery black and his Rolex seemed to catch the chandelier light with every small movement.

"Hello, Mia. You wanted to meet?"

"I have some questions about the business you're supposedly doing with my husband, Serge. Don't even bother trying to deny it. Have a seat."

"I don't know what you think you know, Mia, but it's best you stay out of it," he snapped.

He was about to take off, but I placed my hand on his arm lightly and held him back, waving down the bartender to get him a drink.

"He'll need something strong, Chris, and we may be here for a while," I said assertively to the bartender who knew us all a bit too well at this point. *It clicked that I had not asked Chris any questions at all yet, what did he know? He knows everyone's business. Drunk lips tend to spill secrets.* I made a mental note, but first I had to deal with the highly arrogant Serge.

"Serge, cut the bullshit, please. I have had enough of Aaron's lies. You know something, and I need you to tell me. I need you to remember that Aaron isn't the only one with secrets around here that some people would do anything to keep hidden. I'm sure you're one of them. I know your marriage hasn't always exactly been the cleanest of arrangements."

He sighed, taking a swig of his whiskey before opening his mouth.

"Since when are you the one to play hardball, Mia? You've always been so quiet, so reserved."

"That was before I found out that everything I damn well thought I knew was a lie."

"Your husband has been a very busy man. You may not know every investment he's ever made, but it seems he has chosen wisely. You do know he's invested a lot of goddamn money into Playa Vista Towers, right?"

"No, I didn't. I know he has a lot of deals in the works, but not that any of them were going on here," I said.

"Oh, Mia. You waltz in here with your head held high trying to get information out of me and you don't know what you're even after. If I were you, I'd try to get my priorities in order before I try to break someone."

"I will ask you this once, and I need the truth, Serge. What is Aaron up to?"

"Well, for starters he's moving the office into one of the basement floors. He's investing in developing new apps for some high-profile celebrities, and he's gonna be fucking rich. Richer than he already is, of course. That about does it. I'm surprised you don't know, being his wife and all. If you think

I'm going to talk about Aaron's private business, you don't know me very well."

"Celebrity types?"

"You know, those Youtubers, Instagram Influencers, whatever you millenials call each other, I don't care."

"Like Jade?" I asked.

"Oh yes, they spent loads of time together. Too bad they couldn't make any real money. She just vanished. Typical. Anything else, Mia? Or can I get back to enjoying my day?"

I couldn't say another word to him. It was clear now that Aaron had been harboring the kind of secrets that would break us. He'd been sitting on the truth this entire time and I still had to figure out how to get it out of him.

That evening came and I just couldn't get out of my head. I didn't even notice when Aaron came home. He took me into his arms, holding me tight, like he'd always done, but I felt nothing. I was completely numb as he kissed me, as he believed that everything between us was somehow fine. We were getting ready for bed that night when he got into the shower. I heard the water running and I saw his suit jacket sitting on the chaise lounge near the closet. I pulled out his set of keys, looking at the little tag attached to one of them. *P1 Office. This is it. This is my in. I'll find the truth tonight. I have to.*

Taking the elevator down to the basement office made my heartbeat quicken. It was dark, damp, and exactly the kind of place that needed a vast amount of renovation. I fished around in my pocket for the keys, but before I could open the door, I spotted Nora heading to the elevators from the garage entrance. Nora worked at St. John's in the emergency unit, and she looked exhausted.

"Mia? What are you doing down here at this hour? Going out?"

"Ah, I was just going to grab Aaron's blue Armani jacket. It's in his office," I said.

"Yes, I remember that he's moving his work down here. He didn't tell me much, but the last time I saw him, he had a pretty rough night."

"When was that exactly?"

"It was a few months ago. I came home after a long shift and he looked like he was moving things into that office himself. He cut his leg open pretty badly. Apparently one of his liquor bottles broke. I patched him up and sent him on his way," she said.

"Do you remember what night it was exactly?"

"Ah, I don't think so. Why?"

"Is it possible that it was the night Jade disappeared?"

"Come to think of it, yes maybe it was," she said.

"I'm sorry, Nora. I really have to go."

She nodded with a smile, but I could tell that she felt strange about our little encounter. I unlocked Aaron's office door, rummaging through his things, completely ready to tear the place apart to find what I was looking for. *You had an entire life that I didn't know about, huh?*

I tried to open the side drawer to his desk, but it wouldn't give. I held the bunch of keys in my hand, trying every single one of them until I found the right one. *Bingo.* I reached inside, pulling out a file, a burner phone, and a flask of whiskey.

I sat in his new executive chair, opening up the file, and my heart sank into my stomach. There were endless pictures of Jade, bank statements, and information about her business. It was all right there in front of me. Every ounce of evidence pointed to him, and with every new piece I learned, I began to unravel just a bit more.

I heard rustling coming from outside, and I stuffed everything under my sweatshirt, rushing out of his office before the sound of heels *clacking* grew closer.

"I'm here. What did you need again?" I heard a familiar

Russian voice ask. It was soft, sultry, and I recognized it instantly.

"How am I going to get into the drawer if you can't find your keys?"

I hid behind the corner, glancing over at Irina's expensive cream coat and heels. It dawned on me that she was there helping Aaron, but seeing as how closely involved Serge was, it all made sense. I waited until she was safely inside Aaron's office before I snuck over to the door. I watched her lift a paperweight, grabbing the spare key that was under there. *If only I'd known about that.*

Her manicured fingers wrapped around the handle and she pulled the drawer open, her face riddled with shock.

"There's nothing in here, Aaron. No, you don't understand. It's empty. Whatever was here, it's gone now."

I heard my cell phone start to buzz and I fished it out of my pocket to see Aaron's name light up on the screen. *Shit.* I thought of the first person I could trust, scrolling down my contact's list, sending her a quick text. *Brenda. I hope you're home. I need to crash at your place tonight.*

I headed straight for the elevator when I got the reply. *Sure. Come on over.* I breathed a sigh of relief. I texted Aaron to let him know Brenda and I were too invested in some scary movie. *Will he buy it?* I got up to Brenda's safely, and she had already laid out a new pajama set for me.

"You're a lifesaver," I said.

"Oh shut up. I know you've been going through some shit. This is the least I can do."

Her phone started ringing a few moments later and she answered, but as she did, her eyes sunk to the floor.

"Hello? Aaron? Yes, uh she's right here," she said, handing me the phone.

I mouthed to her to let her know it was okay and I put the phone to my ear.

"Hello?"

"Oh, Mia. I just wanted to make sure you were okay. Have fun. I love you."

You absolute psychopath. I thought, but at least I knew it was easier lying to him when I didn't have to see his face.

"I love you too."

~

I clutched the hem of my glittery evening gown, glancing over at the man on my arm, the one I knew was involved in Jade's disappearance. He'd collected every bit of information about her that he possibly could, each photograph telling its own story, and from the looks of it, Aaron developed some sort of obsession. I knew how hungry he was for the next million-dollar deal, but I was starting to see the lengths he'd go to in order to get it.

We arrived at Regine and Jeffrey's lavish apartment. It was filled to the brim with peonies, their bright pastel colors blending well with the warm light from the chandeliers above. My heart was pounding hard every time Aaron got near me. I smiled as he made small talk with the rest of the guests and pulled me in for a soft kiss ever so often. I couldn't let him know what I'd learned.

My fingertips brushed against my soft updo with a few pieces left out to frame my face. I watched Aaron move through the small crowd of dinner guests. Every single person was someone I'd suspected at one point. He talked, laughed, and continually glanced over at me, probably waiting for the right moment to slip away. Regine came over to chat with me, and she looked truly elegant with her stylish Parisian-style bob haircut, oversized eyeglasses and welcoming smile. She handed me a glass of champagne.

"I'm so glad that you and Aaron were able to join us, Mia. Jeffrey has only ever seen Aaron on the tennis court these days when he's trying to wow his next shark. I know the world is in a state of chaos, but that shouldn't stop us from having a little fun, right? Thanks so much for coming dear, please, enjoy your evening," she said.

She glided away, resting her hand on her husband's shoulder while they chatted with Irina and Serge. I looked around for Aaron, but he was nowhere to be seen. I watched Irina closely, knowing she had a hand in this somehow too. *I saw what you were looking for, Irina. You're not going to find it. Why are you doing this? Why are you helping, Aaron?*

I hid behind one of the large marble pillars at the other end of the room, finishing the rest of my champagne, just as Irina broke away from the crowd. She ventured off down the winding hallways of Regine and Jeffrey's perfect palace in the sky. Their unit was on the penthouse level, with breathtaking views and multiple balconies, including one with its own private plunge pool. The rumor amongst the club was that Jeffrey had sold his company to Google for over one hundred million dollars, and their impressive home seemed to back that up. I followed Irina closely, my heart thumping so loudly I could hear it in my ears, and she turned the corner to a slightly cracked door.

"Are you sure you looked properly? I had my keys in my pocket hours before. I need that stuff back, Irina. If it got into the wrong hands-"

"Maybe your wife is closer to finding out the truth than you think, darling. She could've taken them."

"She's as clueless as your idiot husband. He was a good sport about getting the basement renovations done and my office, of course. Mia is a lot of things, but she doesn't know about our little problem. She's far too concerned about me cheating on her," he said.

"I don't know why you're even still with her, Aaron. She doesn't love you enough if you can't trust her with the truth. I still think you should've taken care of that little problem a long time ago," she said, reaching up to caress Aaron's face.

My stomach turned watching the two of them interact so intimately, but I couldn't look away. Watching Irina's hands on my husband nearly pushed me to my breaking point. I couldn't ignore what was happening right before my eyes, the fallacies unraveling slowly. I was on the cusp of the truth now.

"I'm not a killer, Irina. I'm not just going to kill her."

"So, what are you going to do then? Wait for the cops to show up on your doorstep asking questions? You diverted the attention for months now, Aaron but that won't last forever. I still think Mia may be catching on. It's time you think about dealing with her, too."

I felt lightheaded like I was going to pass out. There it was, the piece of the puzzle that had been missing for such a long time. *Jade's still alive.* I thought, the relief coursing through me, only to be replaced by fear when I remembered what Aaron had said.

"I'll take care of it," he said, getting ready to head towards the door. *What are you going to do, Aaron? Make me disappear too?*

I rushed away from the door, turning the corner, and slipping back into the lively party. I clinked glasses with my friends, had a delicious dinner, and it seemed that with every minute that passed, Aaron grew more suspicious of me. I saw the way he looked at me from across the table, how proud he was to be free, thinking he was getting away with it all, but that would soon change.

You can sleep with Karen and Irina. You can lie to me. You can destroy everything we had, Aaron, but I won't let you hurt my best friend Jade. I will find her. I will put an end to this myself. I'm closing in on you now. You better watch your back.

20

AARON

76 Days Missing

*J*rummaged through Mia's closet, tearing through her designer label clothes, her expensive shoes and handbags, trying to find my things from my desk drawer. Part of me believed that Irina had to be wrong, that Mia couldn't possibly believe that I had anything to do with Jade's disappearance. *Maybe Irina was right, Jade. Maybe I should've killed you the minute you double-crossed me,* I thought. *I had a lot of goddamn money on the line, people surely kill for less.* I glanced over at my bed, watching as Mia slept peacefully with her back to me. I guess she needed to conserve her energy for another day of snooping around Playa Vista Towers. I heard my cell phone ring and I rushed over to answer it so it wouldn't wake her up.

"Aaron? I'm sorry to bother you this early, but the electrician is here to set things up in the storage unit in the basement. It's chain-locked. Do you have the key?"

"Tell the electrician to come back another day. I'll set it up. Thank you, Serge."

"But he's already here. It'll be easier if he can - "

"Just leave it be. I'll handle it. Thank you," I said.

I watched as Mia stirred under the sheets. I hung up the phone, sliding up behind her. She turned around to face me, her eyelids fluttering open calmly, and I studied her face closely. *This isn't the face of someone that thinks I hurt their best friend.*

"Who was that?" she asked, sleepily.

"No one. Just business."

She nodded, tucking her hand under her head, going back to sleep. I noticed that she was still wearing her three carat diamond and also the anniversary band, she wasn't dreaming of a divorce. *Who could replace me in her life? No one.* I made my way out to the living room to check my emails, making sure everything was in order for tomorrow's showing to the investors. I kept my name off of the paperwork when I purchased the Towers, when I had the entire building under my control, and now it was time to show them what I was capable of. *I had to go to extreme lengths to make up for the loss you caused, Jade. I wish things could've been different, but that's the last time I trust an insignificant bitch like you.*

I wished there was someone who could get rid of her for me, take her somewhere where I didn't have to see her again, but that would be too easy. I wanted her to suffer for what she did to me. I wanted her to know that her life as she knew it was over. *It was easier when no one knew what I was doing. Someone knows now. Someone has my file, my burner, and who knows what else? What if they find her? What if they tell the cops?*

I knew it wasn't enough to convict me, but it still scared me shitless. I took a hot shower, calling downstairs for breakfast to be prepared and packed. Mia made herself a cup of coffee, typing away at that laptop of hers, and she seemed relaxed. She was a fragile girl, the mere thought of something bad happening to Jade had broken her, and I knew if she was somehow sitting on real information like Irina suggested she would've gone to the cops by now. *I don't have to worry about her. What I have to worry about is the woman rotting in the basement of my building.*

"Where are you off to?"

"Meetings, Mia. I'll be late again tonight."

"Alright," she said as I leaned down to kiss her.

I thought it was odd that she didn't question it this time, but our marriage was barely hanging on by a thread, and I'd shut down her suspicions. *She probably doesn't want to push me.* I thought. I remembered a time where we were happy. I remembered a time where building a life with Mia seemed like what I wanted. That was before I realized what I wanted most in this world she'd never be able to give me. She operated on her morals, relished in how much of a good person she was. I needed someone by my side that was willing to go to the lengths necessary to maintain my fortune.

That's how real money is made after all. I entered the elevator, heading down to the lobby. The receptionist handed me a full brown paper bag, smiling at me graciously. I took the elevator down to the basement. I felt the sweat trickle down the back of my neck, my hands shaking as I remembered the night this all began. I thought about what it felt like dragging Jade's limp body into that empty, concrete room. I tied her up, taped her mouth shut so she wouldn't be able to scream. It felt good at the moment. It felt like I'd finally enacted the revenge I had wanted ever since I found out what she'd done. It was very unwise to cross me.

I was still lacking my keys and I couldn't find them in Mia's possession. I walked over to the small set of boxes and concrete brick that was left by the builders. It hadn't been touched in a while because I'd halted most of production. Inside the top flap was the spare key to the large padlocked door. I opened it up, hearing groaning from the moment I entered, and I could sense the frustration that'd been building over seventy-six straight days.

The room was dark. I turned on the small lantern in the

corner of the room. There she was, sitting on the single mattress, wearing the new clothes I had Irina bring to her. I placed the brown bag of food down on the small kitchenette counter, turning to look her right in the eyes.

"I brought you something to eat. It's been a while since you had any real food," I said.

She stared up at me with dark-ringed, bloodshot eyes.

"Why bother? Aren't you just leaving me here to die? That's what you want, isn't it?" Her voice was raspy, low, to the point where it didn't even sound like her anymore.

"I didn't plan for this to happen, Jade. If I had it my way, we could've been business partners. You would've had your life, your best friend, and you may have finally had the balls to leave your sad excuse of a husband. Besides, it's not like you're tied up. There's a bathroom over there, a kitchenette. You have a place to sleep. Be grateful." I said.

"You took everything away from me, Aaron, all because I decided not to go with your deal? Am I supposed to be grateful for that?"

"You and I had an agreement! That agreement was supposed to make me six million dollars. You stupid bitch. It was real low of you to make me think you were going to sign the damn contract only to go with someone else. That fucker wasn't going to get you places, Jade. I tried to tell you that, but did you listen?"

"You cornered me in an elevator, told me I was making a mistake the moment you found out I wanted nothing to do with you. Robert told me how you do business, Aaron. He told me the kind of corners you cut to make your next million. I asked you if Mia knew what kind of man you are, and what did you do? You waited until we got to my floor, and you slammed my head into the elevator wall."

"You should be grateful I kept you alive all this time. The cops have lost interest in you, but it took them a while. I did everything I could to point them in the direction of your fucking husband, but they gave up. Detective Blanton gave up on you. Everyone went back to their lives and you became a topic of fleeting conversation. Where are all of your followers now? Not the legacy you were hoping for, huh?" I asked.

She launched herself at me, managing to get her overgrown nails to dig into the skin of my arm, but I pushed her off. She landed on the floor with a thud, but she no longer cried the way she used to. There were no tears streaming down that once beautiful face of hers.

"You try that shit again and I might just have to kill you. I kept you here because I didn't know what else to do with you, Jade, but every day you try my patience. Irina is convinced that I should get rid of you and that I should get rid of Mia too because she can't stop looking for you. Now, the world doesn't care about you anymore. If there was a time to dump you somewhere, it'd be now," I said, with a chuckle.

It was the first time I'd seen fear in her eyes in a long time. She clutched her knees to her chest, trembling. It was then I realized that even after rotting away down here for seventy-six days she still hadn't come to terms with dying. *You probably thought I was too much of a coward to do it, Jade. It doesn't have to be messy. I can slam your head into the wall hard enough and you'll be gone,* I thought.

Jade really was a thorn in my side. I sighed, kicking the brown bag of food over to her so she wouldn't try to attack me again. She didn't open it. She didn't even touch it. I stood back and folded my arms across my chest.

"This may be the last time you eat in a while. I suggest you enjoy it."

"You're not going to get away with this, Aaron. Someone will find me. Someone will - "

"Everyone out there thinks that you've gone off the rails, or that you fled because you couldn't take living with your drunk of a husband David anymore. The only person that thinks differently can't do anything about it. My wife will lose this interest in you eventually, and by then, you'll be long gone," I said.

"You're sick, Aaron. You're fucking sick. How did this happen? We were all friends. I saw you get married. I was there when you two were trying to have a baby. How could you - "

"I can't believe you're still asking that fucking question after all this time. You're the reason this happened, Jade. You're the reason my marriage is over. You're the reason I'm out six million dollars. You just didn't know when to quit, did you? Choosing Robert over me. After everything I did for your career. You'd be nothing without me!"

I rushed over to her and grabbed her by the throat. The anger coursed through me as I squeezed tighter. She tried to fight back but she couldn't. I wanted to keep going, I wanted to put an end to this nightmare, but when the life started to leave her eyes, I couldn't go through with it.

"You took everything I did for granted. You deserved everything you got."

She didn't say another word to me. She curled up in the corner, shivering with fear, and I had to figure out what I was going to do. I was scrambling for a way out of this. There was someone out there who knew what I'd done, and the more I thought about it, the more I wanted to deny it was true.

Mia? Are you the one fucking with me? If I find out that you are, I'll have no choice but to put an end to this. You shouldn't have been snooping. You should've just minded your goddamn business.

MIA

Found

I felt sick to my stomach. My world was crumbling down around me, and there was nothing I could do to stop it. I clutched the ends of the towel to my chest, still dripping from my shower, and I felt like I was on the edge of the truth. It felt so close that I could almost taste it, but for some reason the fear kept me frozen. I sat there alone on my tufted lounge chair in the walk-in closet for an hour, grateful that Aaron had a full day of meetings that would keep him away from the apartment.

He's hiding her. He's kept her alive all this time, but why? I needed to get out of my head if I ever hoped to process what was going on. I got dressed, making my way to the kitchen to make myself a cup of coffee. I spotted Aaron's iPad on the table. It lit up with a meeting notification from his calendar. *Meeting with the Board. Basement Tunnel Reno.* My eyes widened as I took it into my hands, like I'd just found the golden ticket I was looking for. *So, you're building tunnels under the Towers now, are you? What in the hell for?*

I slid up on the screen as it opened to the browser page he'd last been looking at. It had pictures of a speakeasy, and it looked to be some kind of underground getaway. I put it down, tying my jet black hair back, feeling my heartbeat increase. I glanced down at the time to see I only had a half hour before he was going to have this meeting, and I needed to get down to the basement before he did. I grabbed my keys, slipped them into the pocket of my jeans and rushed out the door. *Please be there, Jade. Please. I'm so close now. You have to be alive.*

I pressed the elevator button, watching as the door opened up to reveal Irina standing there with her Chanel slung over her arm. *Shit.* I got inside, clicking the lobby button so she wouldn't think that I was heading back to Aaron's office. Irina would be trouble if she thought it would help Aaron, and who knows what she would try to do to me. Although she could be charming, everyone in Playa Vista Towers understood that she was one cold-hearted bitch. She didn't say a word to me until we arrived at the ground floor, but when she turned to look at me, I knew exactly what was on her mind.

"You may have Aaron fooled, Mia, but you're just as sad, lost, and unlovable as Jade was. It's a shame, really."

"What the hell are you talking about, Irina?"

"I think you know exactly what I'm talking about. I know what you took. It won't be long now. Ta," she said, waving at me.

I waited until she made her way to the automatic doors at the front before I bolted for the stairwell. My ears were ringing as my espadrilles carried me down to the basement where I turned into the hallway down from Aaron's office to the locked room. The lock stood there shining under the single fluorescent light overhead. There was a blue tarp covering the rest of the door, but I needed something to break it.

I looked around, spotting a tool box on the other end of the room near one of the pillars. I rummaged through it quickly, pulling out a pair of pliers, but before I could do anything with them, I heard footsteps coming. I slid between the stack of large boxes that were pressed nearly all the way up to the wall, hoping that no one would hear me breathing.

"This brings us to the end of our tour. Once renovations are complete on the space for the speakeasy, I'll take you through there as well," said Aaron.

"Why can't you just give us a little peek?"

"Because that will ruin all the fun." Laughter.

I peeked out from my hiding spot, clutching the pliers close to my chest, hearing the footsteps get farther and farther away. I took a deep breath, slipping out carefully without knocking anything over in case it made Aaron turn back. I went straight for the door, cupping the curve of the padlock with the pliers, pushing down with every ounce of strength I had, but it wouldn't break. I tried again. I tried once more, propping myself up against the surface of the door. The pressure from my fingers felt like they were going to break, but with one last push, it broke. It fell to the floor with a loud *clang!* and I glanced over my shoulder to see if anyone was coming.

I waited a minute in the deafening silence, then opened the door slowly. My heart was beating so fast at the thought of what I may find. I clutched the pliers closely, fumbling around at the front of the door for a light, and when it finally came on, that's when I saw her.

She was sitting in the middle of the small basement room, the windows barely letting in the slightest bit of light. There was a single mattress on the floor, a small kitchenette, and a bathroom. There were bags of new clothes from the boutique in the courtyard, and I imagined Irina brought them down here herself. She looked up at me, probably expecting Aaron because I saw how still her eyes were until she realized I was the one standing in front of her.

"M-Mia?"

"Jade! Oh my God!"

I rushed to her side, my hands shaking, but I tried my best

to keep them steady long enough to help her up. I wrapped my arms around her, the pliers falling to the floor with a loud thud.

"I can't believe it's you. It's really you."

I felt the tears well up inside my eyes, and I pulled out my cell phone to call 911 when Jade's expression changed.

"Mia! Behind you!"

I didn't even get the chance to turn around. Aaron's big, bulky hands wrapped around my throat. I dropped my phone. I felt the lightheadedness start to set in. I tried with every ounce of strength I had to fight back. Aaron slammed me down on the concrete floor. He started pacing.

"I told you to stay out of this, Mia. I made it real fucking clear you shouldn't have gone snooping. Now, I have to take care of the both of you. It's over now," he said. I could not believe the flatness of his voice and the detached and cold stare he was giving to both of us, like we were just two strangers on the street.

I got to my feet and punched him straight in the jaw hard enough for a little bit of blood to spill from his lips. I tried to reach for my phone, but it was no use. Aaron pushed me to the floor again, his hands wrapped around my throat.

"J-Jade," I said.

I turned to look at her. She was completely frozen, barely able to stand. Once she saw what Aaron was doing to me, she leaped into action. I could see that the anger she'd been harboring for more than two straight months had resurfaced. I was counting on it. The world around me had started to fade to black, but as my eyes struggled to stay open, I heard a loud thump. I looked up to see Aaron's eyes shutting, the blood trickling from his head, and his grip on my throat finally loosened.

He fell to my side completely unconscious. Jade rushed over for my cell phone and dialed 911.

"Hello, I'd like to report a kidnapping and an attempted

murder. My name is Jade Richardson. I'm being held against my will in Playa Vista Towers. Help!"

I heard the scrambling on the other end of the line as the operator promised to get units there right away. Jade told them where we were. She dropped the phone the moment she was finished. I wrapped my arms around her, holding her tight.

"You came for me," she said.

"Of course I did, Jade. I never stopped looking for you. I never stopped believing you were okay."

"I'm not okay Mia. But thank you. Thank you for saving me."

We were both completely sobbing now. I glanced back over at my unconscious husband, the man I wanted to start a family with, the man who had nearly destroyed me. *How could I have been so blissfully ignorant for all of these years about his true nature?*

"It's over now, Jade. It's over."

I heard yelling coming from down the basement hall, and right as the cops entered the room, Aaron's hands grabbed a hold of Jade.

"Y-You bitch."

The cops surrounded him. They put him in handcuffs. He spit blood onto the floor of his perfect little concrete cave before they hauled him away. I was shaking, completely in shock, but I suddenly felt incredible relief. Despite the trauma I'd faced, and discovering the ruthless ambition and cruelty of the man I had loved and trusted, I did it. I saved my best friend. I did what I'd promised myself I'd do and now she was safe. Now, we were both safe.

In the end of this nightmare, at least we have each other. We have the chance to change our lives now. The world will know what happened here today and it won't be splattered in some meaningless news article where our voices are lost. They'll hear it from us.

EPILOGUE

JADE

here in the world am I now? Everything around me changed in an instant. The world has become an entirely different place, but I seemingly didn't mind. I sat on Mia's beautiful living room couch with a cup of tea in my hand and a blanket wrapped around my shoulders. For a few weeks after coming out of that dungeon, I considered moving out of Playa Vista altogether. Instead, Mia persuaded me that David should be the one to pack up and go. I wasn't sure if I would ever feel safe here again, the way I had when we first moved into this tight-security luxury building. Knowing that all of my dearest friends live here ultimately convinced me to stay. Besides, if a person you believe is a friend is going to betray you, no amount of security cameras can protect you, and I found that out the hard way. It made me less excited about sharing the details of my life with strangers on my Youtube channel, but I still needed to make a living.

Mia and I sat in a comfortable silence while I read the stack of pages she had printed and bound, the story of the man who nearly destroyed both of our lives. I relived every aching memory, every painful reminder that I was closer to death than I ever wanted to be again. There were moments in that basement where I asked myself whether I should end it all, but I didn't want to make things easier for him.

He was riddled with fear at the thought of having to be the one to kill me. That wasn't because he was afraid to do it, he was afraid he'd get caught. I didn't want him to die. I wanted him to feel every ounce of pain and suffering I did being treated like an animal. He would rot in jail for the rest of his life and I'd get the fresh start I'd been dreaming of for the last seventy-seven days. It was all thanks to Mia. She never stopped looking for me. She never stopped believing I was out there somewhere.

"So, what do you think?"

"I think it perfectly captures everything. The thought of me having to sit and click on my camera to talk about it all was too much to handle. This is exactly what I needed. Thank you, Mia. Thank you for everything."

"I'm just glad you're okay. There are also a few people here that are dying to see you," said Mia, her face lighting up the entire room.

"Bring them in," I said, with a chuckle.

In came every familiar face I remembered, every neighbor and friend from our Playa Vista Social Club, with the exceptions of David, Irina, Serge, and, of course, Aaron, who would be sitting in a jail cell for a long, long time.

My true friends were all in a state of shock and joy all at the same time. It brightened my day to have everyone gathering in my honor. It made me feel like there really was a new beginning on the horizon. I found myself laughing, giggling, and excited to start living fully again. It was the first time in ages I experienced real happiness. I was surrounded by love: real, unconditional love. Everyone that had made my life a living hell wasn't here anymore. They had to take it up with the police about the hand they played in nearly ruining my life.

I no longer had to worry about the dark, twisted ways of those that wanted to cheat their way to the top. I turned a fresh page, thought about this chance to explore the limitless possibilities of what life had to offer, and I didn't have to go after any of it alone. I had my best friend by my side, and we had lots of genuine sincere friends right here in this little paradise. Finally, I had my life back. I am a survivor. I know what I am made of and that nothing will break me.

Made in the USA
Las Vegas, NV
21 December 2024

15078505R00125